NEXT DOOR to THE SUN

NEXT DOOR
TO THE SUN

STANTON A. COBLENTZ

Wildside Press
Berkeley Heights ◆ New Jersey

Wildside Press
P.O. Box 45
Gillette, NJ 07933 USA

NEXT DOOR to THE SUN

CHAPTER I

"There! Down there, Roy! Don't you see it shining?"

"Lord, Chris! It's like a star that goes on and off!"

Through the tiny tinted quartz portholes of the spaceship *Rocket Age,* the sun stared huge and monstrous, so brilliant that the two men could hardly look at the spots of light it cast on the ship's gray inner wall.

Beneath them to the left, they could see a mighty globular surface, most of it with a glare as of molten metal, though part was cut off by a band of blackness, as of a moon not quite at its full. Field glasses had shown the men the flashing light near the borders of the black region.

"That smooth shining round patch near the light —what's that?" gasped Roy Bentley, a lean six-footer, with large, light-blue eyes, flowing flaxen hair, and a

seven weeks' growth of flaxen beard. "Why, it's as
even as the bottom of a bottle!"

Chris Hartridge, flashing his electric blue eyes and
giving a toss to his carrot-red mane, let out a low
whistle. "Couldn't be natural," he mused. "Not pos-
sibily. Maybe, after all, some of the people of Mercury are still alive!"

They both, of course, knew the main historical
facts. A little more than five centuries ago, the Earth
had been devastated in the Hydrogen War, which
had been fought by two great groups of nations, led
by America in the west and Russia in the east. After
a barrage of hydrogen blasts, the original nations had
ceased to be, and the world's population had dropped
ninety-five per cent.

But perhaps not quite ninety-five per cent had
perished. Amid the panic of the last days, tens of
thousands had sought other planets in the space-
craft then in assembly-line production. Unfortu-
nately, the Russians had been first to Mars; and the
westerners, accordingly, had aimed at Venus and
Mercury. From the pioneers to the former planet, no
word had ever come to Earth; but many ships had returned to report the safe arrival on Mercury of thousands of men, women, and children, along with
freight and provisions.

This, however, had been more than five hundred
years ago, back in the dying days of the twentieth
century. Soon afterward, new hydrogen blasts had
disrupted all attempts to communicate with the ad-

venturers. And the war's survivors and their descendants had been too busy trying to keep alive to give much thought to Mercury.

But now, with the revival of science and of space-flying, a great question was being asked. Might some descendants of the original space-travelers not survive? Mars and Venus, unhappily, had yielded no evidence; and few expected any results from little Mercury, flying at hardly more than a third of the Earth's distance to the sun, with one face perpetually sun-baked and one face eternally frozen.

Recently, however, a new interest in Mercury had stirred two young fliers, honor graduates of the celebrated Einstein Space Academy: Roy Bentley and his chum, Chris Hartridge. They had little difficulty in inducing the World Space Authority to commission a visit to Mercury, to seek word of the lost explorers. After all, why object if two twenty-three-year-old daredevils, unmarried and otherwise unattached, chose to risk their lives in the interest of science?

So now at last, after months of preparation, they were within reaching distance of Mercury—actually whirling around it at the speed of a satellite. And already they were making discoveries: first, that weird light sparkling starlike every now and then from Mercury's surface; and next that queer round patch, which they had just photographed.

"You know," concluded Chris, tugging thoughtfully at his ragged red beard, "it couldn't be ice.

Natural ice has all sorts of bumps and hummocks. Besides, see how beautifully curved this is, just like you'd cut it with a chisel. I'm all for a closer look!"

Dashing to the controls, he gave a turn to the atomic motors. Soon that smooth shining patch was staring beneath them again, partly in sunlight, but largely in shadow.

At the same time, the flashes from below had become brighter, more frequent.

"Notice that, Chris!" Roy pointed out, bumping excitedly about the twelve-foot confines of the ship. "They come in a regular sequence, three short and a long, three short and a long, three short and a long! Here! Let's make an experiment!"

He pressed a button, and a brilliant shaft shot from the searchlights on the vessel's prow. He pressed a second button, and the searchlights went out. Four times he repeated the act, each time allowing the searchlight to burn for two seconds, and finally for about ten seconds.

He had hardly finished when the mysterious light again appeared below. In about two seconds, it flashed off. Then four times more it went on and off, then shone steadily for ten seconds.

The men stared at one another; for a time, both were speechless. "Maybe we're balmy with the confinement," muttered Chris. "But suppose we drop a bit lower."

At their new height of twenty-five miles, the smooth, glassy region seemed to cover hundreds of square miles. A small part of it, edging into the planet's sunlit side, had a bluish tint, a little like sea water; the remainder cast an odd, steady glitter.

"Whatever it is," concluded Chris, knitting up his bushy brows, "darned if I can explain its luster. Starlight isn't half bright enough to account for it."

Roy banged against an instrument panel in his eagerness for another view of the strange patch. "Why, it's translucent!" he broke out. "Light comes up from under it!"

They were now curving and spiraling about the glassy region, like a hawk circling its prey. For several minutes, they had no further clue. Then, in the midnight darkness at the curved borders of the mystery region, a battery of lights flashed on, fifty or sixty in all, with colors varying from rose-red and ruby to emerald, orange, sapphire blue, amber, purple, silver, moon yellow, and pure blazing white.

"Don't you notice, old fellow?" Roy burst out, brushing a lock of his long flaxen hair back from his eyes. "They're—they're the form of a letter M!"

Petrified, the two men stared and stared.

"What the devil can it mean?" Roy threw out, after a minute. "But of course, M stands for Mercury!"

"Also for Murder! But maybe it's a W upside down."

"All the better. W is for Welcome."

"Also might mean War! Or Warning!"

"Warning or Welcome, Chris, it's up to us to go down and find out."

Chris wiped an invisible sweat from his craggy brow. "Just the same, old fellow, I have a funny feeling there's something waiting down there that we won't be glad to meet. However, it's too late now to turn tail."

To alight on solid ground would be difficult and dangerous. The *Rocket Age* had to descend very gradually, approaching the surface at an angle of not more than five or six degrees, while decelerating by counter-rocket blasts. As Mercury was airless, wings would be of no value; but on the other hand, no heat would be generated by friction with an atmosphere. But in order to avoid disaster after their speed would no longer hold them up, they had to cushion the jolt of landing with huge, specially prepared springs, along with shock absorbers made of a substance like foam rubber, though much tougher.

Having picked a smooth-looking landing field several miles from the great M (or W) of colored lights, they clamped themselves in their seats, and awaited the inevitable shock—which jarred them into unconsciousness. But after a few seconds they revived, unclamped themselves, and rushed to the portholes.

"Strange," remarked Chris as he pointed out at the icy ridges glittering in the starlight, "here we're right next door to the sun and might as well be in the Antarctic."

Minutes later, they had adjusted their spacesuits, which made them look like deep-sea divers, yet rested on their shoulders like feathers, since gravity on Mercury is less than a third as strong as on Earth.

Then silently—for the spacesuits prevented speech —they passed through the *Rocket Age's* triple doors, which enabled them to leave and enter with minimum loss of oxygen. At last they were on the planet's surface, reeling just a little beneath the dark bulk of the spaceship, which stared at them like a monstrous bullet turned on end.

An uncanny stillness hovered everywhere. And as they turned the flashlights about them, all that they saw was ice, broken only by a pyramid of rock more than a hundred feet high, perhaps a fifth of a mile to the right. To the east there was a faint glow from the mysterious colored lights. High above them the untwinkling stars, vivid with a pinpoint brilliance unknown on Earth, shone in their familiar constellations. Far to the left blazed Venus; and still farther to the left, not so bright as Venus, was a beautiful double planet: the world they had left seven weeks before, and its companion the moon.

But they had no time for sky gazing. Their problem now was a practical one: how cross the ice fields toward the colored lights?

Then, as they stared at one another blankly, terror shot over them. From across a ridge of ice not a mile away, a sparkling light arose. Instantly it was followed by a cigar-shaped form, perhaps thirty feet

long, faintly luminous, and with six thin legs dangling below, and two orange-red searchlight eyes in
front.

At unbelievable speed, by prodigious hops, it
dashed forward in parabolas each hundreds of feet
long.

The two men could never say which was the first
back into the spaceship. As they crowded one another
to the door, their only thought was to be inside, start
the motors, and get away.

CHAPTER II

"Curse that lever! If I'm not the world's prime idiot!" groaned Chris, gray and aghast.

"What is it!" demanded Roy. But he saw that Chris, in his panic, had pulled the Detachment Lever by mistake, cutting off the motors. And now the Automatic Shut-Off System, designed to prevent anyone from being accidentally caught in the power field, would keep the motors out of action for an hour.

A long dismayed second passed while the men stared at one another, still in their spacesuits, though the helmets had been thrown off, permitting speech.

"Just our luck!" Chris muttered. "But let's not lose our nerve!"

He dashed to a porthole, fastened his eyes to the narrow strip of quartz, and let out a cry that brought Roy instantly to his side. For a fascinated moment, both were speechless.

On the icy plain, only a hundred yards away, the

hopping monster had come to rest. Its searchlight eyes no longer shone, but its six legs had been folded beneath its luminous body, and its cigar-shaped bulk rested on the ice. A large egg-shaped patch at its side shot open, and two strange creatures glided out. They were clad in bearlike, vaguely luminous suits. Their faces were covered by some transparent reddish substance. They did not walk, but moved by leaps.

"Pinch me hard, man!" mumbled Chris. "Am I dreaming?"

One of the creatures, lifting one hand and pointing a finger-long tube toward the ship, flooded the whole scene with unbearable brilliance.

"They're taking flash pictures!" Roy shouted.

"I'd give my right arm for a flash getaway!"

Chris bent down, turning the switches to reactivate the motors. "Maybe in an hour, with luck—"

But a yell from Roy drew him back to the porthole.

One of the strangers had come across the ice halfway to the *Rocket Age*. He stood stockstill, motioning with one thick, bundled arm—motioning first to the ship, then to the luminous cigar-shaped vehicle.

"He's telling us to come out and join him in his hopping monster," interpreted Roy.

"Does he think we're plumb loony?"

"I wouldn't say so," denied Roy, sharply. "We two ought to be ashamed of ourselves, Chris, being such scary sisters—"

The creature had stopped motioning; with one

long spring, he had reached the spaceship. There followed a series of heavy thumps on the door.

"He's knocking to come in!"

"Must suppose we haven't the brains of a fly!"

The thumps continued, louder, more insistent.

Then the creature himself could be seen just outside a porthole. Roy found himself peering, at a distance of two feet, through the stranger's red transparent covering into a human face. Oddly, the face was smiling!

"You know, Chris, he looks friendly."

Chris took a peek, and concurred. "What do you say to lettting him in?"

"How do we know it's not all a ruse?"

The rapping at the door continued.

"Why should it be? Besides, aren't we two to his one? How can we establish contact if we don't let him in?"

Chris mumbled something that sounded like acquiescence. Roy, after stripping off his spacesuit, touched the automatic door opener.

An anxious minute later, the stranger strode in, bearing with him a faint odor as of burnt rubber.

His first gesture, after the doors had swung shut behind him, was to get down on his right knee and swing his right arm in a wide arc, with such a quaint courtesy that the watchers exchanged amused glances.

Then, back on his feet, he pressed a button somewhere in his clothing. His face-covering peeled off, revealing a bald man, with a small, round, wax-pale countenance, domed and wrinkled forehead, pudgy nose, and tiny gray-green smiling eyes.

"Welcome!" he broke out, in understandable English, but with a strange accent—a sort of mealy foreign-sounding mumbling. "Very long we have waited. Welcome, my good mennen, to our planety Mercury."

The hearers had trouble not to laugh. Chris held out his hand, which the stranger ignored, while addressing all his remarks to Roy.

"We welcome you, too," said Roy—at which the stranger's face was twisted as if he also wanted to laugh. "But don't you mean, your 'planet Mercury' and 'My good men'?"

"I mean not so! 'The planet Mercury'!—I could say it not. We have used not that form for four hundred years. The same with that barbarous 'men.' We say 'women' and 'children.' Why not also 'mennen'?"

As the absurdity of this came to Roy, he could not keep back the threatened laughter.

"I have the much great honor," went on the little man, "to message you from the Bureaudent—"

"Who in fury," asked Chris, "is the Bureaudent?"

The speaker cast him a scornful glance, and went on, still to Roy. "Most well esteemed sir, the Bureaudent, he asks you with us to come in the Practigard—"

"Practi what?"

The speaker stepped to a porthole, and motioned

toward the huge cigar-shaped machine. "To come in the Practigard inside the Plastidome. You will there be honored with fitting ceremonialings."

"But who are you? What is the Plastidome? Who are your people?" asked Roy, though he felt he could answer the last question.

"I am not one of the Public Informationers. I speak not on state matters. Put on your space suiters. Fear not anything! We are friend people!"

Roy hesitated briefly, then said, "Thank you. We're glad to accept your invitation."

"Be damned if he can lure me!" snapped Chris.

"He's not trying to lure you, old man. Can't you see? These people sighted us from far off and signaled us to come down. And we—we ought to get down on our knees and give thanks! Don't you understand, Chris—these are the lost Earth-people!"

"I'm not blind. Fact that they speak English—of a sort—is proof enough for me. Still, Roy, I've a feeling I'll be sorry if I do go—"

Roy had reached for his spacesuit.

"As for me, I'd never look myself in the face again if I didn't go. You stay here, if you prefer—"

"And have you think I've got the yellowest liver that ever went on a space flight? No, damn 'em!" growled Chris, fumbling at his space garments. "You can count on another passenger in that Practi—what does he call it?—that Practigard!"

CHAPTER III

"Before we leave, most esteemed mennen, let me myself introducize. My name, it is Hennery Jon-ess."

"Pleased to meet you, Henry Jones," acknowledged Roy, holding out his hand, which the stranger heartily shook, while protesting, with a frown, "No, not Henry Jones. That—it is the old-fashioned style. The modern form, it is Hennery Jon-ess."

Roy apologized, and mentioned his own name, which Jon-ess called "deliciously quaint." But when Chris introduced himself, Jon-ess appeared not to see him.

"Now," said Jon-ess, "to the Practigard let us go."

Clad in their spacesuits, they covered the short distance, Jon-ess hopping across the ice, while the others followed more slowly. The second native, who was still waiting outside, bowed in the same odd way as his countryman. Then Jon-ess motioned the newcomers into the Practigard through a triple series of doors, which opened automatically on contact, and automatically closed behind them.

"Whew!" Chris muttered, when they were safely inside. "Sure is rigged up de luxe!"

The whole passenger compartment, about fifteen feet long and seven high and wide, was filled with fluffy artificial-rubber pearl-colored pillows, which were piled high as seats and were fastened even to the ceiling, where several triangular patches gave out a milky illumination. A series of small oblong windows, with pale-blue plastic panes, marked both sides of the compartment.

Jon-ess and his guests removed their spacesuits and took seats on the pillows while the other man went into a forward compartment to operate the machine.

Almost at once, they started off, shooting up on a hundred-foot arc, and coming down with what would have been a bone-jarring jolt except for the pillows. Sometimes the passengers' heads bumped the ceiling, and sometimes Roy and Chris sprawled forward on the floor.

Jon-ess meanwhile apparently used to this sort of ride, never for a moment lost his balance. "After a while, mennen, it will bother you not any more," he promised, a twinkle in his gray-green eyes.

"Where the devil you taking us?" grumbled Chris.

Jon-ess did not answer. But after a time they saw for themselves. In a mighty line ahead, beyond the eerie glitter of the ice fields, they could observe the great smooth area that had surprised them from above. Its outer wall, curving so gradually that it looked straight, rose out of the frozen wilderness as high as a skyscraper. By a faint bluish light that penetrated the wall, they could see great pipes, thicker than a man's body, which stretched along the ground and entered the wall; and above the wall was a multitude of wires, tied and twisted in bows and knots, woven in meshes like gigantic cobwebs, coiled and braided over immense parallel rods, or drooped toward the roof of the main structure with loose ends dangling.

"That, it is the Plastidome," explained Jon-ess. And just then they came down with a jerk that threw Roy and Chris across the floor.

At the Plastidome, the Practigard stopped briefly. A section of the wall, as of its own initiative, closed behind them, and they found themselves in a low tunnel, beyond which another large gate opened for them automatically. Beyond the second gate there was a third and a fourth, separated from each other by tunnels.

"Reminds me of the locks in a canal," remarked Roy.

"I know not what you mean," answered Jon-ess, laughing. "Locks are hair. How can a canal have hair? These doors, they are all needed, so that the air of the Plastidome, it may escape not into the death world."

The hearers took it for granted that, by "death world," Jon-ess meant the entire planet outside the Plastidome.

Having passed the last gate, they were in an enclosed region, so immense that it hardly seemed enclosed at all. In front of them, and on all sides, at intervals of several hundred yards, Titanic pillars branched upward, seemingly of metal, tinted a pale blue, and rising four or five hundred feet toward a ceiling, also pale blue, which gave the illusion of an actual sky. The light, however, did not come from the ceiling itself, but from innumerable geometrically shaped patches—bluish or milky white illuminated squares, circles, triangles, rectangles, pentagons, and hexagons, which shone in strips of various sizes from the branching pillars and the cement-like floors and pavements.

All this came to the observers only by confused glimpses. "Lord, it's worse than a circus!" Chris muttered. And just then the Practigard began hopping along a wide avenue lined with barrack-like three-story stone houses, with queer V-shaped and W-shaped windows.

This, evidently, was a central thoroughfare, for it was filled with swarms of Practigards. Most of them were much smaller than the one carrying the Earthmen, being but eight or ten feet long, and many were partly open. They were of various colors—purple, yellow, crimson, golden, snow white, jet black, grass green, or striped or spotted—and each had two blinking searchlight eyes. All had legs instead of wheels; all moved by hops and jumps; all would briefly touch the pavement, spring along in the way of a running cat, then leap forward scores or hundreds of yards at heights of anything from ten to fifty feet. There were so many of them, and they veered and curved so sharply, and came so fast and from so many directions, that it seemed miraculous that they did not constantly collide.

"What do you call this place?" Roy asked Jon-ess.

"What you think we call it? Can you see not? We are inside the Plastidome."

Suddenly the Practigard turned at a right angle and dipped to the floor, making Roy and Chris once more lose their balance, while another machine, whirring like a buzz saw, flashed by them an elbow's length above.

"Wow!" muttered Chris. "That was darned near our finish!"

But Jon-ess looked as unperturbed as ever.

"Where—where you taking us?" Roy jerked out.

"We go," answered Jon-ess, in matter-of-fact tones, "to the Octagon near the Rhomboid."

When the hearers laughed at this, Jon-ess rebuked them sharply. "What you mennen find so funny? The Octagon, it is a public assemblifying place, named for its shape. The Rhomboid, it is the palace of the Bureaudent, also named from its shape."

"Why are you taking us to this Octagon?" Chris asked Jon-ess.

But he seemed not to hear.

"Why are you taking us to the Octagon?" repeated Roy.

"We take you because many people, they wait there to see you. The Air Voice, it has told them that you come."

"Is Air Voice your name for radio?" Chris asked. But again their host seemed deaf to his words.

Jon-ess went on to say that his people had known of the spacemen's approach at a thousand miles: sensitive antennas, on the upper surface of the Plasti-dome, had caught the stirrings from outer space, which had been confirmed by telescopic observations. And so they had flashed on the lights in order to signal the spaceship and guide it safely down, and had formed the blazing M to designate "Mercury."

"Everybody, they are much eager to see you," Jon-ess went on. "They gather in the Octagon. After that, you go to the Rhomboid to meet the Bureaudent."

"Sure looks like we're nosing into high society," mumbled Chris. "But will this crazy ride never end?"

They traveled for miles. The territory changed; the avenue widened, and was flanked on both sides by grim identical granite structures, as high as ten-story skyscrapers, but windowless, flat-roofed, and as flat-looking as packing cases.

"How you like?" asked Jon-ess, with an air of pride. "This, we call it modern architecting."

At last the flight was drawing to a close. During a long final hop, they looked out across an eight-sided open space, a hundred acres in extent, at least ninety per cent occupied by parked Practigards, ranged in concentric circles, one above the other, seven stories high. Most of the remaining ten acres were packed with humans, who were waving long triple-forked pink banners and shouting uproariously. At one side stood a large stone platform, with two room-sized enclosures behind it, each leading to the street by means of a winding stairway. And the largest pink banner of all shone above the platform.

"Out now we get," said Jon-ess, as the Practigard jarred to a halt in an open space that had been cleared near the platform. "The people, they want to see the first mennen who came from the planety Earth in five hundred Earth years. They want you should to them talk."

"Good Lord!" Roy groaned to Chris. "Are we expected to make a speech?"

CHAPTER IV

"Say, just look at them, old fellow!" Chris whispered as he followed Roy and Jon-ess up the platform stairs. "What do they think we are? Tigers in a circus?"

But he could not make himself heard against the cries of the multitude.

"O-way! O-way! O-way!" The cheers rang out, volley on volley. "Way-o! O-way! Way-o! Wheek! Wheek! Wheek!"

Almost in a solid body, the people were pressed together. Over in the distance, at one corner of the Octagon, there was a wild surging and scuffling, where some late arrivals were trying to force an entrance and were being thrown out by some dagger-bearing guards in green tunics.

Glancing out over the crowd, the Earthmen saw that most of the people were small and lean, about the size of average Japanese, and with thin, spindly legs. Their complexions were pale, almost waxen; and close to half of them were bald. Men and women alike were dressed in tunics that stopped at the knees, leaving the calves bare above rubbery-looking sandals; and the tunics were of every hue. One thing which both Roy and Chris noticed once more was the odor, as of burnt rubber.

On the platform, about twenty persons were seated in a semi-circle, on three-legged golden-cushioned chairs, just under the huge pink banner. But upon the arrival of the visitors, all arose, got down on their right knees, and raised their right hands in token of salute.

"O-way! O-way! Way-o!" they still cheered, in an ear-splitting din. "Wheek! Wheek! Wheek!"

As the visitors took the seats proferred by Jon-ess, their eyes wandered to one end of the semi-circle of cushioned chairs, and they caught sight of *her*— caught sight of the girl with the sea-blue eyes, the long drooping pale lashes, and the hair as flaxen as Roy's own.

She could not have been more than about twenty-two, was taller than most of her people, and was dressed in a white satiny tunic. Her blonde, small-featured face made a perfect oval, and a whimsical smile played about the well-formed, unpainted lips. And when Roy chanced to catch her eyes, she smiled back with a naïve, gentle sweetness.

Nevertheless, she had no smile as she glanced at

Chris; instead, the suggestion of a frown puckered her dainty face.

"Good God, old man, what've I done?" Chris whispered to his partner. The fact was that nobody on the platform had a welcoming smile for him, though all were beaming upon Roy.

A wrinkled, bald-headed dignitary arose from a seat in the center of the semi-circle. He raised two knobby hands, and immediately the crowd became quiet. Roy and Chris saw thousands of pairs of small eyes, baby-pale or doglike or weasel-dark, staring at him curiously.

"Fellow Mercurites, mennen and women," he said, pressing against a railing, and swinging two bare sticklike arms, "my duty as Head Planicrat, great pleasure today it gives me. For now the space barrier, it is not any more."

"O-way! Way-o! Way-o! Wheek! Wheek! Wheek!" shouted the crowd.

The Head Planicrat now spoke so fast and mumbled his words so badly that Roy and Chris could make out nothing at all. The difficulty was increased by the amplifying system, which brought the speaker's voice back with such reverberations that he seemed to be mocking himself.

His remarks, as later translated to Roy, were as follows:

"Fellow Mercurites, this is the day we have long awaited. As you know, it is five hundred and three

Earth years since our forefathers left the Earth with nine hundred and eighty-nine spaceships, most of them making ten or more round trips, to transport eleven thousand people and their supplies. Of these, six thousand perished; but the survivors, with magnificent courage, threw up the first rude Plastidome and roofed it with a translucent plastic to keep out the dreadful cold of the Mercurite night, the dreadful heat of the Mercurite day, and the deadly ultraviolet rays and the X rays from the sun.

"I need not go into details: how we met our needs by means of atomic reactors from the Earth; melted the ice from the planet's frozen side, which supplied inexhaustible water; dissociated some of the water by electrolysis, to release oxygen for breathing and produce our atmosphere with the addition of chemically generated nitrogen; and made food synthetically from rocks and water, creating starch and sugar through photosynthesis with the aid of artificial sunlight, while protein was supplied by certain fungi grown in caves.

"All this is an old, familiar story, as is the fact that we have prospered, extended our Plastidome to cover more than twelve hundred square miles, and grown in numbers to more than three hundred thousand. I need not remind you, also, that with all our progress, we have felt one great lack: in all these centuries, no word has come from our mother planet. We have been unable to establish contact, and though we have never ceased to search the skies for space-ships, none has ever reached us until today.

"Wise men have therefore taken for granted that which our ancestors feared—that the madmen of five centuries ago exterminated all life on Earth. But we could not go down to find out, since all our space-ships had long ago crumbled to ruins and we had not the means to make and operate new ones.

"There has, however, remained a legend that some of our brothers, having escaped atomic destruc-tion, remained on Earth and, after many years, would fly up to Mercury and crown us with blessings. More than that! The commander of the space fliers, our special friend and protector, would be a giant, the Light Bearer, with blue eyes and flowing hair like flax.

"Behold, therefore, fellow Mercurites! Let me introduce our Earth brother, the man of the legend, the Light Bearer, who has come to shower blessings upon us! I believe he has a message for you."

"Way-o! O-way! Way-o! Wheek! Wheek! Wheek!" screamed the crowd, swinging their pink banners exultantly.

Roy meanwhile, having let his glances stray to the lovely girl of the sea-blue eyes, was startled to feel someone prodding him from behind, and to see all eyes fastened upon him.

"You're in for it now, old pal!" he heard Chris foretell. Then he felt one of his hands grabbed by

Jon-ess, who had taken a seat just to his right, and found himself being jerked to his feet and propelled toward the railing.

"Way-o! Way-o! O-way!" the people kept applauding. "Wheek! Wheek! Wheek!" And the pink banners swung wildly.

Then, swaying slightly and a little dizzily, Roy was alone at the railing. A terrifying silence settled down as he saw innumerable small pale faces staring up at him expectantly.

"Ladies and gentlemen, I come here—" he began with an effort.

Commencing close at hand and traveling swiftly to far parts of the audience, a rocking, shaking blast of laughter halted Roy in mid-sentence.

Red-faced, he wondered what he had done wrong. But no doubt the phrase "ladies and gentlemen" was obsolete. Should it have been "ladies and gentle-mennen"?

"Women and mennen, my name is Roy Bentley," he tried again; paused briefly; then went on more boldly. "I come here, as you know, from the planet Earth—"

Now the laughter began all over again, louder and longer-lasting. And Roy realized what he should have said.

"I bring you the greetings of the planety Earth," he corrected himself. And then, remembering that Chris had always been known as a good speaker, he thought of a gracious way out of the ordeal. "Now I want to introduce my pal, Chris—Christopher Hartridge."

Darting back to his grinning partner, he seized his arm, and half coaxed, half pushed him forward.

Strange and unexpected was the response as Chris stood before the railing, his electric blue eyes flashing, his carrot-red hair and beard seeming almost afire in the reflection of the numerous lights. Chris could actually feel the antagonism, a wave that struck him almost with physical violence. He could see the contraction in the nearest faces, the dark and sullen looks; could hear the cries that began at the furthest corners of the Octagon, and, with mounting fury, were taken up by every part of the assemblage. "Whoo-whoo! Whoo-whoo! Whoo-whoo! S-s-sh! S-s-sh! S-s-sh!"

"Shucks! I've sure messed things all up. But can't imagine how," Chris whispered into Roy's ear when he had plummeted back to his seat. "Better take over for me!"

Just then, from loud-speakers placed high on all the Octagon's dozens of great roof-supporting columns, a thunderous chorus broke out in song:

> "The pick of all the worlds are we!
> Give thanks, good friends, give thanks to be
> The chosen folk of Mercury!"

There were fifteen stanzas, after each of which the singer halted, while the people bawled the refrain with such gusto that Roy's ears ached.

Then, during a pause between stanzas, Jon-ess tapped Roy on the shoulder and passed him a thin white wire, capped by a pearly bead no larger than a bean. "Here, take this. Hold it near your ear. When you another speech make, repeat the words it to you says."

Roy did not know how thankful he was to be for the wired bead.

After the song, the Planicrat once more took the platform. "Again we hear from our friend with the quaint name, Roy Bentley, one of the great men of the planety Earth!"

At the platform's edge, Roy swayed and felt like falling over. How could he say that he was nobody at all on the Earth? He was afraid of using the wrong words; but there was that bead, which he had placed near his ear. Some voice which it carried was saying to him, "Ready! Begin!"

Then, in clear, slow syllables, it dictated his speech.

"Most noble Mercurites, from the planety Earth I come to you good mennen and women to message you with friendship. As everlasting as the Plastidome are the bonds between our planetys. We make salutings, and many kind wishes we bring. . . ."

In this vein the speech rattled on and on, Roy somehow managing to repeat most of what he heard. Every once in a while, following the instructions over the wire, he would pause; and then there would be uproarious applause.

Almost exhausted from the long day's efforts, Roy thought that the speech would never end. But on and on it rambled, saying the same thing twenty times, in twenty ways. His head began to reel; he clutched at the railing for support. Finally he felt himself pitching forward. He tried to steady himself; then, while the roaring of the multitude thundered in his ears, everything went blind and blank. . . .

CHAPTER V

When Roy came back to himself, there was still a roaring in his ears. But there was something else, a sense of rapid, inconceivably rapid motion. He opened his eyes in terror, and saw nothing. The roaring seemed to increase. Then he had the feeling of diminishing speed, and was dazzled by a bluish blaze, and shaken by a sharp jolt. A transparent lid above him lifted itself off, showing that he was in a coffin-sized steel container.

As he staggered to his feet, he found himself inside a large, blue-walled, blue-lighted room. There was still that odor like burnt rubber. Just beside him, a grumpy-looking Chris was lifting himself out of another coffin-like container.

"Thank the Lord, we're out of them!" Chris muttered, pointing to two dark circular caverns in the wall, each about three feet wide. "I had hardly room to breathe in. That guy Jon-ess calls them Tubelators."

"Tubel what?"

"Tubelators. Pneumatic tubes that carry passengers and freight. I thought we'd never get out alive."

"I—I must have blacked out," gasped Roy.

"Sure did. They put you in the Tubelator, saying it was guaranteed to bring you to." Chris hesitated, took a nervous stride about the room. "Hell! Nice mess we're in! Rummy speech you made, too."

"It wasn't my speech," defended Roy, as he slowly came back to himself. "I simply spoke what they told me to."

Chris ran one hand crisply through his tangled red hair. His blue eyes crackled. "God, man! Have to be a parrot just because they ask you to?"

Moodily Chris ranged across the large, bare room, whose stone floor was covered with a green, mossy-looking mat.

"This whole blamed planet," he complained, "is the crummiest place I've ever seen! I'm in favor of making a beeline back to the spaceship."

"Oh, come now, give them half a chance!" Roy expostulated. "Anyway, we can't turn back now."

"No, dammit, sure looks like we're caught!" grumbled Chris, still ranging impatiently to and fro.

Even as he spoke, they heard a crashing from one of the circular wall cavities. A partition shot open, a coffin-shaped container clattered to a halt, and Jon-ess, looking as unconcerned as ever, popped out.

"Ah, I knew you mennen would be waiting here in the Rhomboid," he said as he stepped on a lever, causing his container and the other two to go rattling back into the wall.

"I was by the Circulators detained," he explained, smiling amiably out of his tiny gray-green eyes.

"Who the devil are the Circulators?" snapped Chris.

"Who the what? I know not what you mean by the devil. No, now I remember. He was a character in the mythologizing of the mennen of old."

"But who are the Circulators?" Roy asked.

"Have they not then any Circulators on the planety Earth? They are the—well, the mennen and women who the big news tell to the Air Voice and the Daily Sheets."

"You mean, reporters? And newspapers?"

"I know not those words. But you will see. You must with them have an interviewing before you go to the dinner which the Bureaudent gives to honor you."

"Glory!" Chris muttered into Roy's ears. "We're in for a full schedule!"

"Listen here, Mr. Jon-ess," Roy appealed, "we both need a rest. We're hungrier than wolves. Need a bath, too—haven't had a chance at one for seven weeks. Also, a razor might help with these weeds on our faces."

"A razor—no, not yet. The Bureaudent, he has

ordered that we must leave you looking as quaint as when you came down. Afterwards, we will give you civilizated clothes."

"You mean, civilized?"

Jon-ess threw Chris a scornful glance.

"Come here! You may a bath take in the Spraye-leter."

He snapped open a door, and seemed surprised that neither visitor knew anything about the Spraye-leter, which operated by drenching the bather with a warm perfumed spray. Having explained how to regulate it by means of electric switches, he rushed on, "You now one minute excuse me. I go to speak with the cooker."

"Oh! The cook?" corrected Roy.

"No, the *cooker!* The man who cooks! When I speak of him who bakes, I call him not the *bake!*"

Crushed by this logic, Roy made no reply.

"Either everybody else down here is crazy, or I am!" Chris decided, as he and Roy stood in the spray of the bath together. However, after the bath he felt much better, particularly as Jon-ess soon returned with a little self-propelled wheeled table covered with food.

They lost no time in taking seats about the table, though Jon-ess did not join in the repast.

"Now these, they are the best synthesized eats," he explained, seeing that the visitors appeared puzzled by the viands, colored every bright hue from scarlet to emerald, and cut into various geometrical shapes.

"This"—he pointed to a pyramid of golden jelly—
"it is mock roast. That purple cone, it is mock salad.
This yellow coil, it is mock bread. That bluish spher-
oid, it is mock pudding—"

"For Pete's sake!" Chris whispered to Roy. "Everything seems to mock something!"

Being famished, they lost no time about digging
in, though the mock soup tasted like water seasoned
with straw, the mock potatoes were like putty, and
the mock steak had the flavor of rock.

"Great wonders have we done with out food," explained Jon-ess. "Our scientitioners, they tell us that
our food, which by chemistry they make, it is more
wholesome and good to the taste than anything on
the planety Earth."

"Sure is room there for a difference of opinion!"
Chris mumbled as he struggled with a stringy mass
that threatened to choke him.

Now the visitors thought they knew why the
Mercurians—or Mercurites, to use the local term
—were all so small and waxen-pale.

However, the two men managed somehow to
make a meal. They had not quite finished when they
heard a banging at one of the doors, giving place to
a series of thumps, and then to shouts and yells.

"What's the riot?" asked Chris, pushing away a
plate filled with red globules that looked like cher-
ries and tasted like glue.

"Riot? We have not any riots. We are civilized
people. It is only the Circulators, who have their

patience lost, and come from the Circulatory Hall."

Meanwhile the thumps, shouts, and yells continued. And suddenly the door burst inward with a crash, admitting a wild-looking crowd, who swarmed around the visitors as if to tear them limb from limb. Simultaneously, scores of lights flashed like superbrilliant fireflies as the intruders pressed the bulbs of dime-sized cameras (which, by a process of enlargement, would give pictures of any size).

"Tell us your story! Tell us!" they screeched. "For the Air Voice! . . . For the *Golden Sheet!* . . . For the *Carmine Sheet!*"

They were pressing in so closely that it was hard to breathe.

Dominating the invaders was a broad-limbed woman, with a blade-shaped face, protruding nose, and chin as angular as a hawk's beak. Somehow, she managed to reach the Earthmen just a fraction of a second ahead of the others.

"I am Marigold Har-reys, of the *Purple Sheet,*" she introduced herself. "I want to questionnaire you!"

She had addressed herself to Roy; Chris she ignored.

"Your name, sir?" she demanded, in a voice as rasping as a file.

"Roy Bentley."

A ripple of laughter traveled through the room.

"Roy?" chortled Marigold. "Roy? There is not any such name!"

"No? Well, guess again. It's from the French—original meaning was 'king.' "

"King? King?" several voices echoed. "That is a much good name! King Bentley!"

"Now, King," Marigold went on, while all the others took out faintly glowing card-sized notebooks and began scribbling with sharp bits of metal, "now, King, what is the name of your fellow traveler over there?"

Without even looking at Chris, she jerked a scornful finger in his direction.

Indignantly Chris's voice roared out. "If you want to know about me, lady, *I'm* the party to consult!"

A sultry flash lighted Marigold's small dark eyes. She thrust her thin pointed face forward as if to impale someone, then addressed a fellow Circulator in a screech that everyone could hear.

"As if anybody ever imagined I was a lady!"

Not until later did Roy and Chris understand the point of this. The word "lady" had changed in meaning, and now applied only to women leading a loose life.

"What's your name?" one of the male Circulators asked Chris, looking at him obliquely, as if committing an offense against morality.

"Christopher Hartridge."

Again a ripple of laughter.

"How long did it take you, King, to get here from the planety Earth?" Marigold resumed, turning back to Roy.

"My name is *not* King! It took seven weeks."

But he had to explain what he meant by "weeks," a word no longer in use. The hearers did, however, understand the meaning of "day," since they still followed old habit and divided time into twenty-four hour units, although the actual day on Mercury was eighty-eight times longer than on earth.

Questions now began flying so fast that Roy could not keep up with them; half a dozen Circulators were crying out at once. Why had he come to Mercury? What had he expected to do here? How did he like the planet? Why had no one else come for five hundred years?

With his poor command of Mercurite English, Roy struggled hard to answer, and was wondering how to escape when a gonglike sound boomed from a loud-speaker on one of the walls.

"Mennen and women," a voice crashed forth, "it is time for the Grand Receptioning by the Bureaudent preceding the Banquetication!"

Instantly, as if forgetting all about Roy and Chris, the Circulators started for the door. Marigold again was first, while the others almost tripped over their own heels as they pushed and shoved their way out.

"We go with them," Jon-ess informed Roy. "We take the Tubelator up to the Receptioning Room."

CHAPTER VI

The hall was as large as a city block. It was crossed with twin rows of columns curved in the Grecian style, but undecorated except by blue light patches that covered them in geometrical shapes. From the ceiling, forty feet above, varicolored plastic globes dangled like huge clusters of grapes, each ribbed and spotted with light strips; and light strips marked the sides of the ventilating tubes, which entered from the roof like the downturned funnels of ships. The floor, of inlaid stone, was carpeted with a springy plastic decorated with pictures of suns and planets. At one end of the hall a crescent-shaped table, large enough for a thousand guests, gleamed with a pale blue covering and a glitter of crystal utensils.

As Roy entered, he heard a great babbling of voices, noticed the familiar odor of burnt rubber, and saw hundreds of persons, all in bright-colored tunics. Dozens surged forward in the hope of being introduced, but from the beginning he had eyes for one only.

With a stab of joy, he saw *her*—the girl of the sea-blue eyes, the long drooping pale lashes, and the hair as flaxen as his own. She was glancing toward him as he arose from the Tubelator—and did he only imagine that her smile was friendly?

"Who is she?" he asked, nudging Jon-ess. "Couldn't I get to know her?"

Jon-ess's face was crossed by a slight frown.

"It will be not easy. But I will try. Many would like to know Verne Wyle, the Bureaudent's only granddaughter."

"Bureaudent's granddaughter?" gasped Roy, seeing a wide abyss open up between him and the girl. "Still, I've got to know her."

Jon-ess began weaving his way toward Verne. Roy saw him go down on his right knee, and wave his right arm in token of respect. He heard her laughter tinkling forth. Then Jon-ess motioned to him.

The girl held forth both her hands to Roy in a formal Mercurite manner, and he took them with a bow that she must have considered very quaint, for again he heard that laughter tinkling.

"I never thought I would any mennen meet from the planety Earth," she said, looking up at him with a beaming smile on her perfect little oval of a face. "Tell me, what is it like on your planety?"

This gave him his chance. Differences in lanaguage seemed not to matter; her eyes were fixed on him in absorbed interest as he attempted a description; they exchanged constant smiles; and he quite forgot the people about him, quite forgot the great hall, quite forgot that he was an Earthman and she a Mercurite.

Then, many minutes later, he felt someone jostling him, and heard a voice in his ears. "Much pardon I make, King, but I must another question ask you." And as Verne slipped away, Roy found himself staring into the cold blade-shaped face and hawk eyes of Marigold Har-reys.

He hardly heard her question, but shook her off with some made-up excuse. And as she bored her way back into the crowd, it came to him that, since arriving in the reception hall, he had seen nothing of Chris. But there he was, slouching in a tired manner at a side entrance. Roy noticed that the people shrank away from him as from a snake.

"Where've you been, old sport?" Roy asked. "Exploring?"

"Should say so!" Chris pursed his lips, as if he had chewed by mistake on a bitter almond. "Somebody, in his rush, shoved me into the wrong Tubelender—"

"Tubelator."

"Who cares what you call the contraption? Anyway, I came out in some sort of a cellar, where a couple of wolf-dogs wanted to take the seat out of my pants. I've been wandering around for an hour; hiked up about ten stories, and was lost a dozen times before I heard the big noise from this direction. It was harder than a space flight!"

Chris mopped his brow and sank down on a long bench, whose further end was promptly deserted by three Mercurites.

Just then a bell sounded, followed by a voice from the loud-speakers: "Mennen and women! The Banquetification begins! You will all your seats take at the table!"

There was a flutter and a rush as everyone surged towards the table. Above each of the hundreds of chairs, a flaming red sign shone with the name of a guest. There was some confusion, of course, but in a few minutes everyone had found his seat. Roy saw that his name—"King Roye Ben-tlie"—had been flashed at the head of the great table, between two signs that read, "Joa-seph Wyle, Bureaudent" and "Will-burr Why-te, Head Planicrat."

"You're sure getting into swell company," commented Chris, "but where do I go?"

They scanned the hundreds of signs, but could not discover Chris's name.

"We must our apologizings make," they heard a familiar voice as Jon-ess, perceiving their confusion, came up from behind.

"You come this way," he went on, flicking a finger toward Chris, who followed him to the further end of the table, nearly a block away. Roy saw Chris take a chair; but did not observe how, a moment later,

the men to the newcomer's right and left arose and
withdrew.

Roy was now introduced to the Bureaudent, a but-
tery-looking man about five feet tall, with a bland,
round face on which a perpetual grin seemed pasted.
His colorless eyes, above bags of fat, were dull and
inexpressive; his chin was barely noticeable; and
his low forehead was overtopped by a reddish pate.
His skin, less waxy than seemed usual among his
countrymen, had a yellow tinge; his voice reminded
Roy of smooth, soft soap. He seemed immensely
popular and was the center of a buzzing crowd.

As they took seats, Roy saw that the right side of
the table was reserved for men, and the left side for
women. At the head of the fair ones sat "Mad-lyn
Why-te, Women's Plaincrat." She was stationed just
above "Eye-leen Ell-ey-yott, Chairodent of the Daughters of the Plastidome," a fat, aging creature with a
sharp, cleft jaw above her double chins. And the
chair just to the left of Miss Ell-ey-yott was taken
by Verne, who sat smiling happily at Roy out of her
lovely eyes.

But a rattling from below distracted his attention. Peering down, he saw a small platform stretch-
ing about ten inches under the table, with miniature
steel rails about six inches apart. On these rails, carried by tiny vehicles like flatcars, the dishes of food
moved in an automatic procession, stopping before
each diner for a few seconds. Roy was to learn that

you had to help yourself without hesitation, or the food would go clattering away.

"Before eating, we will all some Vitosan enjoy," remarked the Bureaudent, beaming at Roy.

Bottles of a bubbling pinkish fluid came rattling along the tracks, and the Bureaudent helped himself liberally, and filled a generous glass for Roy.

"What is it?" asked the guest, smiling expectantly. "A sort of wine?"

"Wine? Wine?" snapped the Bureaudent, his face losing its grin. "What mean you? Oh, yes, now I remember. It was an old-fashioned alcoholic drink. Vitosan, it is much bettter; it puts you in the right mood so much quicker. Come! let us good drinks make to our two planetys!"

He lifted the glass, and drained the contents at a gulp.

Roy tried to do likewise, but one taste was enough. The liquid had a flavor like furniture polish and seared his mouth like acid. He gasped, coughed, choked, sputtered, turned red in the face, and lowered the glass, still three quarters full.

"I—I—I can't make it—the taste—"

"Taste?" demanded the Bureaudent. "Who drinks Vitosan for the taste? You swallow it so fast you notice not the taste. Here! I will show you!"

With a dexterous jerk, he seized Roy's glass. A second later, it was empty.

"Ah!" he said, smacking his lips. "That takes practice!"

To Roy's relief, no more liquid was forced upon him. But he was to hear it whispered that his inability to drink Vitosan proved the inferiority of Earthmen.

Even the women, he saw, swallowed the vile substance with the skill of connoisseurs. And men and women alike, after the second or third glass, were enormously enlivened, and began laughing, jesting, and boasting in boisterous tones. In fact, two men at the far end of the crescent indulged in so loud an argument that a pair of green-clad attendants, armed with daggers, had to escort them out.

"Wonder how Chris takes to Vitosan?" Roy reflected. But glancing across the room, he saw his partner sprawled on his chair, his legs stretched before him, his head thrown back, his mouth wide open, enjoying a hearty sleep. The other diners had cleared a circle ten feet wide about him.

"Tell me, Your Honor, what has my friend done to make everybody avoid him?" Roy asked the Bureaudent. "Has he broken any law?"

The Bureaudent gave his face an annoyed twist. "He has broken not any law. But can you see not? Are you color-blind?"

"What's that got to do with it?"

"Well then," the Bureaudent went on, in his mealiest voice, "maybe to your attention it has come that his hair—I like not to say it, but his hair, it is red."

Roy stared at the Bureaudent with the suspicion that Vitosan had gone to His Honor's head.

"It is something we wish to talk not of," the Bureaudent resumed. "But I see you know not about it. Let me with you go back more than five hundred years, to a time just before our ancestors left the planety Earth to escape the Hydrogen Death. There was then a great dictifier who ordered the explosions that killed so many mennen and women—"

"Dictifier? Is that the same as dictator?"

"Dictator is the quaint old form of the word. The dictifier, he was named Nicholas Koskuff. He was the monster that ruined the planety, and his hair was red like fire. Ever since, our people, they have liked not mennen and women with red hair. Such mennen and women, they are treated not like people. They are called Koskuffs. No good citizen with them will associate. They bring not good luck. They are permitted not to marry, and therefore they are dying out. We see not many redheads any more."

"But, heavens!" Roy broke out, indignantly. "Poor Chris can't help his red hair!"

"We can help it not, either. So with him we associate not."

Roy stared dismally across the hall, where Chris was still sprawled, snoring away.

Now, for the first time, the Head Planicrat, who had been busy with Vitosan, seemed aware of Roy.

"I can to you tell something more about these Koskuffs," he said. "Being Planicrat, I see the people much. My business, it is to overlook them and see that they are in a good state of mind and body—"

"But how about the Bureaudent? What's his duty—"

"He is our great leader. His duty, it is to be the first man of all the bureaus. He had not anything to do with anybody's state of mind or body," patiently explained the Head Planicrat, with a wrinkling of his high forehead. "But about the Koskuffs. I know how strong the feeling against them is. They can go not to the Octagon or other public places. They can eat not at tables with regular people, or live in the same houses. Some time ago, a little girl with red hair, she was stoned for wanting to play with some other children. A man with red hair, he took poison; he cared not to live in a world where he could with no one talk. I myself have no prejudice. Of course, I associate not with Koskuffs. But I have not any feeling against them. After all, they are human."

"Believe me, they are!" mumbled Roy, while hearty notes of song came from a party of Vitosan-drinkers at the far end of the table. "Well, guess nobody will have anything to do with me, either, I'm sure not going to forsake Chris!"

"Oh, no, no, your case, it is different!" the Bureaudent and Planicrat assured him in one voice.

"You see," the latter went on, "as I said at the Octagon, the people, they think you are the protector that the legend told of, the Light Bearer with blue eyes, and hair like flax who would come someday and many blessings shower. I myself, I am enlightened; but we the legend tell to the people, for we stay not

in politics if we tell them not what they like. Roy
King, the hero of the legend, he can do not any
wrong. To him anything, it is permitted, even to be a
friend of Koskuffs."

"Well, that sure makes things easier," grunted
Roy, as he dished himself out some food that looked
like roast beef but turned out to have the flavor of
cotton. "I'll have to ask you to treat Chris just like
you do me—"

But neither the Planicrat nor the Bureaudent
seemed to hear. The one was gustily scooping up some
slimy greenish disks from the train under the table;
the other was busying himself with something on a
tiny special platform, also under the table—a little
machine smaller than his palm, equipped with
buttons, wires, glittering metallic reels, and spools of
yellow thread not much wider than a dime.

"Soon," said the Bureaudent, "I must a speech
make."

Some time later, when dinner was about over,
the Planicrat introduced the Bureaudent through a
loudspeaker that blared like a foghorn: "His Honor,
the Right Estimable Joa-seph Wyle, our most distinguishified Bureaudent, will now to you speak with
his well-known brilliance."

The Bureaudent, like the Planicrat, did not rise—
that would have been considered undignified. He
merely cleared his throat, and pressed a button on
the machine hidden under the table. And instantly
the spools of yellow thread began spinning, and a

voiced boomed "Mennen and women, great pleasure to me it gives on this honorfying occasion——"

The voice had exactly the soft, soapy quality of the Bureaudent's. But Roy saw that Wyle was not actually speaking, merely moving his lips.

Every now and then, however, he would press a button on the hidden machine and the voice would make way for the cheers of the audience. And when the cheers had died down, Wyle would press another button, and the speech would continue.

"Clever little inventioning," said the Planicrat in muffled tones to Roy, while the address droned on and on. "This string recordifier, it is wired to loudspeakers all over the hall. The people outside, they can listen by the Air Voice. The recorded impressions, they are magnified ten million times. Of course, our Bureaudent, he has no time to speak his own orationings."

"But isn't that his voice?"

The Planicrat thrust himself far back in his seat and smiled knowingly out of two little weasel-dark eyes.

"That's just it. The people, they think it is his voice. We hire the best actors, who for many days train to be Spectral Speakers——"

"Spectral Speakers?"

"Just so. They practice to sound exactly like the Bureaudent. Many spools of thread they record, speaking the words written by the Spectral Policy Makers. Then the Bureaudent, he hears all the threads, and picks the best. Or if he is too tired, I pick the best for him."

"O-way! Way-o! O-way!" thundered the applause. "O-way! O-way! Way-o! Wheek! Wheek! Wheek!"

CHAPTER VII

The festivities were drawing to their close. Several speeches had been made, including one by the Head Planicrat, who had made use of the "string record-ifier." Then there was another gay round of Vitosan-drinking, followed by the singing of a popular song, which began:

> To Mercury, our hope and home,
> We pledge allegiance through the years,
> Secure beneath the Plastidome,
> The heavenly first of all the spheres.

Roy, rising, edged toward Verne, who had been eyeing him with a faint but friendly smile. He saw her standing among some women six or eight feet away, and was trying to think of something apt to say when the Bureaudent, as if suddenly hatching an idea, seized him by the arm.

"Listen, my good friend! A request I would of you make."

"Go ahead."

"What mean you, go ahead? I stand still now—why must I go ahead? But let me say what I want. You know that nobody, in more than five hundred years, has come down before you from the planety Earth."

"I know that."

"All this time, we learn not anything that on Earth has happened. Our Air Voice, it will carry not that far. So we want to know about the history of your planety for these five hundred years. We want you should write this."

"Me? Write history?" gasped Roy. "Good Lord, I'm not a historian. Or a writer, either."

The Bureaudent raised both hands reassuringly.

"Our writers nowadays, they know not anything about writing. You tell your story to our trained Word Chiselfiers. They take it down on string record-ifiers. Out of it they make a book, and on it your name is put. Our best authors, they all make books like that. I myself, I have made seven. Well, how you like the idea?"

"Can't say I'm exactly crazy about it. What do I know about history?"

The Bureaudent shook his head protestingly.

"Oh, no, surely you know much. What countries there are now on the planety Earth. How they have grown since the Hydrogen Death. What wars they have fought. How people on Earth live today."

"Well, any Earthman could tell you some things you don't know. But it's a heavy assignment, Your Honor. We can't stay on Mercury forever, much as we'd like to," Roy pointed out, casting a glance of longing at Verne, who still hovered almost within arm's reach, chatting with her women friends. "Our people are waiting for us down there. We can't radio them at this great distance. If we stay away too long, they'll think we're lost."

"Oh, no, you must stay a long time," protested the Bureaudent. "But your friend the Koskuff, he can go back."

Glancing at a bobbing flaxen head, Roy hardly heard these words.

"I will some Word Chiselfiers appoint for you," the Bureaudent decided, his colorless eyes taking on a glitter behind their bags of fat. "Oh! You? What do *you* want?"

He had wheeled about to address someone who had thrust herself in from behind. And once more Roy was aware of the blade-like face, the long protruding nose, the sharp, angular chin of Marigold Har-reys.

"Ah! King Roy!" she greeted him, in disregard of the Bureaudent. "You must come right away! I have some Virolife pictures to show you of scenes on the planety Mercury. I myself took them for the *Purple Sheet*."

"Why, I—thanks, not just now," Roy stammered, wondering how to refuse her again without violating Mercurite etiquette. "There are—eh, some other things—"

As he saw how penetratingly her hawk eyes bored into him, he knew that he was making a poor job of his refusal.

Fortunately, the Bureaudent, who was glaring at Marigold, came to the rescue. "Now as for Virolife pictures," he broke in, "the best ones on the whole planety, they have by my granddaughter Verne been taken. Did I myself not appoint her the State Virolife Photographier?"

Hearing her name, Verne had flashed the brilliance of her sea-blue eyes full upon her grandfather.

"But I know not if she would like to show them to the young man from the planety Earth."

Did Roy only imagine that a faint blush overspread the lovely face? But the girl's voice, after a second's hesitation, came forth clear and earnest even if a little subdued. "Oh, yes, Granner, I would be glad to—for the sake of the country—if the young man wants to see them."

"I would be flattered," Roy hastily put in.

"Humph! Her pictures, they are not any more good than mine," rasped Marigold, retreating with upthrust chin and blazing eyes.

"It is late. You can show not any pictures today," decided the Bureaudent, noting that Roy was pale from fatigue. "Tomorrow, Verne, you show him the Virolife."

"Can you come at the sixteenth hour?" asked Verne, with a beaming smile. "Take Tubelator Seven. Forget not. I will be waiting."

"The Head Planicrat, he will a Housing Place show you," said the Bureaudent. "If you think your friend the Koskuff must lodge with you—oh, well you may have him. But I—I advise against such a bad example."

"The question now," said Roy, "will be to find him."

Accompanied by the Planicrat, who had difficulty to keep up upon his spindly legs, Roy wove his way among the knots of people that still crowded the hall. But he saw no Chris. "Most likely the poor devil got tired, and simply went wandering away," he thought.

But just then he saw a red-haired head shooting up from under a table.

"Sure is a neat gimmick, that train on tracks," Chris greeted Roy, with a grin. "Been trying to fig- ure out how she works. I see that by snapping that little wire down there, you could cut off everybody's dinner."

The Planicrat looked shocked, and glowered at Chris.

"Had to have something to occupy me, didn't I?" Chris confided to Roy. "All those speeches put me to sleep. But I give these Mercurites credit. They've sure got the mechanical know-how."

"Also, we have got the see-how," amended the Planicrat, still frowning at Chris. "Now, if you will come, I will find for you a Housing Place."

Though Chris proposed walking, the Planicrat insisted on the Tubelators as the only "civilizated" transportation within the buildings and between adjoining buildings. After a crashing ride, they emerged in a wide corridor, paved with an odd bluish stone, and roofed with curved, silvery sheets lighted from within.

"Ah, here we are," said the Planicrat, pausing just beside the Tubelator entrance, at a door marked "E 119."

He pressed a button, and the door swung open, revealing a bare interior, its outlines just visible by the light from the corridor—a rectangle about ten feet by fifteen, with a floor that seemed either of stone or cement, no windows, and no furniture.

"For Pete's sake!" muttered Chris. "How's a fellow going to stretch out in this rabbit burrow?"

"It is not a—what you say?—a rabbit burrow," denied the Planicrat hotly. "It is the latest, modernest housing on the planety Mercury."

Reaching inside, he pressed a second button, and the room burst into light, which radiated down from platinum-tinted ceiling strips. He pressed a third button, and the opposite wall split open, making way for a W-shaped window. He pressed other buttons, and panels in the wall drew apart, and two beds slid out. A panel in the ceiling opened, and pillows dropped on the bed. Other wall panels clattered apart, and a closet appeared; chairs, a bureau, and a small table emerged; rugs unrolled on the floor; a whirring and swishing of air told that the room was being heated and ventilated; a wash basin unfolded, and a door with the placard *"Sprayeleter."*

"You will be the guests of the Bureaudent," the Planicrat said to Roy. "We hope you will with us many days remain."

"Now here are some monies," he went on, as if suddenly remembering something important. "The Bureaudent, he will for each of you provide ten Mercures out of State funds every twenty-five days."

From a pouch hidden in his garment, he drew an assortment of plastic disks, ellipses, hexagons, octagons, rectangles, and equilateral triangles, colored various hues from ruby red to apple green and saffron, and stamped with faces which, he said, represented various high officials of the State.

"The triangular red ones are the Mercures, the units of value," he explained. "The others, they are worth one twelfth, one twenty-fourth, one forty-eighth part of a Mercure. See! the values are stamped on them!"

The two beneficiaries expressed their thanks.

"You will need not many monies. In the morning,

if you are hungry, there is the button, marked
'*Morning Break.*' "

The Planicrat went down on his right knee and
waved his right hand before Roy in the conventional
gesture of politeness. Then automatically the door
opened—and he was gone.

CHAPTER VIII

"Deep inside me I've got a sneaky feeling we'd better beat it out of this planet just as fast as we can," said Chris next morning as the two men stepped out of refreshing baths in the Sprayeleter.

"What's your rush, you old whirlwind?" Roy demanded. "I'm just beginning to get the hang of things here. Say, when is the sixteenth hour?"

"You've got me there. But since when, old man, is the hour down here so important to you?"

Remembering the Planicrat's instructions, Roy pressed the button marked *"Morning Break."* And immediately they heard a clicking and a rattling; a little door in the wall shot open; and after about a minute, a closed container glided in through a pneumatic tube, and opened of itself, disclosing a steaming broth and various highly colored gelatinous masses of food.

"Well, take me along if you've got any dates,"

Chris twitted. "There was one of those dames that, believe me, I wouldn't mind saying hello to."

"Oh, you mean the old warhorse with the hatchet face? Maybe I could fix things up for you, old chap."

"Kind of you. But I wouldn't cut you out. Say, let's try this!"

He had observed a small notation on the wall, *"Air Voice,"* and beneath it a switch, with "Silence" printed to the left, and "Sound" to the right. And immediately he turned it to the right, and they heard a speaker's heavy, even tones:

". . . widely acclaimified. The man from the planety Earth, whose name is King Roy, he has a private interviewing given to the Circulator of this station. We have this most exclusive storifying. Our Circulator asked: Was he really a king on the planety Earth? Was he also the giant of the old legend, the Light Bearer, who would come here and our people bless and protect? We have the most great happiness to say that the man from the planety Earth, he said the rumorings misled us not—"

"The damned liar!" Roy broke in, shaking his fist at the perforations on the wall, from which the sound was issuing. "I never said anything of the kind!"

"The man from the planety Earth, he to our Circulator says he with us will stay always . . ." the voice droned on.

"Well, this only bears out all that I've said," contended Chris, while he probed doubtfully at a purple breakfast jelly. "Better clear out before we're trapped for keeps. But why didn't the broadcast even mention me?"

"Station G 17. Your Real Truth Station," the voice rattled on. "It is now two minutes before the fifteenth hour."

"Fifteenth hour?" reflected Chris, consulting his wrist watch. "It's about nine A.M. now. They must figure their day from six P.M.—about theoretical sunset time."

"Say, I've only got about an hour before I meet her—" Roy broke out; then stopped short, and bit his lip in embarrassment.

"Ah, old fellow, I admire you! You're sure a fast worker," Chris gibed. "Well, now I see why you begin to like this planet. Good luck to you, you old Lochinvar. And my regards to *her*."

"I'll probably be back—oh, about the eighteenth or nineteenth hour," surmised Roy. "What will you do meanwhile?"

"Me?" Chris paused, and whistled softly. "Oh, there's plenty to do. Maybe I'll try a little exploring. When you get back, guess we'll have some notes to compare."

Stepping out of Tubelator Seven, Roy found a corridor like the one he had just left, with walls and ceiling of some silvery metal, and floor of blue stone. There were rows of doors, some of them triangular, and some rectangular, with crescent tops; but they were all closed. Had he come to the wrong place?

Then suddenly he saw her coming out of one of the triangular doors. She waved to him, and smiled. "You are a little early," she said. "The Virolife Projectory, it is right here."

"Okay," agreed Roy. But she looked at him queerly, as if she had never before heard this expression.

The Projectory was a long, deep room, bathed in an agreeable half-light. It had no furniture, except a large table, a high chair near the door, and the twin telescopes, each about a yard long, which rested on the table and pointed toward the bare metal plates of a wall twenty-five feet away.

"Maybe you have Virolife on the planety Earth?" she asked, with an arch-glance of those sea-blue eyes.

"Afraid not," he answered, thinking that he had never before heard such a soft, silvery voice.

"With the Virolife, we need travel not. It is more good than travel. And much more easy," she bubbled on. "You see, first we run a film along that wall."

She pointed to the wall opposite, and pulled a switch. Instantly Roy heard a faint whirring. But he saw nothing except some minute shadows, no wider than his thumb, which flickered against the wall in a long, straight line.

"Now get on the chair. Put your eyes to the Spectro-Viewers."

He climbed on to the high chair, and she helped him to adjust a chin-piece to the telescopes.

"The Spectro-Viewers, they must focus on the film," she explained, while a little wheel moved the telescopes slowly up and down. "I move the film along the wall. They magnify the film one million times. Ready, Mr. King Ben-tlee?"

"Call me just Roy. Mind if I call you Verne?"

She bent her head from him. In the half-light, he could not see her blushes. But he heard her voice, clear and soft as ever. "Verne, it is my name. Why should you call me not by my name?"

"Good. Verne's a swell name."

"Now I show you the Virolife," she rushed on, with what he considered unnecessary haste. "First, I show you the Outer Plastidome."

Again she pulled a switch. And Roy, as he stared through the twin telescopes, saw an altered world— seemed actually *in* an altered world. All about him it was dark. Overhead, the stars burned in bright, unwinking myriads. Faintly glittering to his left were enormous ice fields, hummock piled upon hummock, glacier upon glacier. To his right, a dim curving mass rose far above, penetrated from within by silvery and golden flickers—the Plastidome! Between him and this structure, several human figures, looking scarcely human, moved beside a parked Practigard. They were dressed in monstrous, faintly luminous suits, capped by transparent, reddish face coverings, and they walked about slowly, examining the base of the Plastidome with blue, red, and yellow electric torches.

"Those mennen, they are the Plasti-Protects," Verne informed him. "They protect the Plastidome. Always some of them, they look to see it gets not any leak."

"How can it get any leak?" Roy wanted to know.

"It happens not often. But we can say not when a meteor, it may hit the Plastidome. There are not so many meteors here as around the planety Earth. But even one could most great danger bring."

"Should say so," agreed Roy. "How'd you handle it if a fireball broke through?"

"There are not any fireballs, for we have not any atmosphere. If a meteor comes through, right away the alarm is given by a system of wires, which penetrate all the plasti-substance. Our whole world, it is made alert. Everybody runs to their stations. We must find out fast where the damage is, otherwise, our air, it all rushes out, and then—"

"And then, good-bye Mercury!" Roy concluded for her. "But even after locating the hole, how do you plug it up in time?"

She explained that all thousand-acre sections beneath the Plastidome were provided with airtight plastic partitions, which ordinarily were folded invisibly against the ceiling, but could be swung into place instantly by the pressing of a button. Thus the damaged area could be sealed off, permitting repairs before any other territory was badly affected.

"But do meteors ever break through?"

"Not often. Last time, it was long before I was born. Still, we must be ready. We know not what day it may happen. Now here—here, Roy," she hastened on, "I show you other scenes on the Virolife."

The next views were fascinating. He saw the huge power plants by which heat from the boiling side of the planet was converted into electricity, which melted the icepacks of the frigid side, and so supplied all necessary water and oxygen. He saw the food factories, several square miles of them, where artificial suns produced starch and sugar out of water and carbon dioxide. He saw the "growing strips," where formless masses of protoplasm throve on a chemical diet, generating nitrogenous foods. He saw the "mushroom caverns," where edible fungi were grown in immense quantities. He saw the "mock forest," a park of five hundred acres, covered with artificial palm trees, pines, eucalpyti, rose bushes, dahlias, and grass that looked exactly like actual growing things. He saw the mines whose electronic equipment was digging out and crushing the rock in great cavities beneath the ice sheets, producing iron, aluminum, copper, zinc, and other metals. He saw synthetic clothes woven and plastic furniture made on block-high automatic machines; and he viewed the mile-long factories where Practigards were turned out by scores of thousands of workers.

"Our chief industry, it is to make Practigards,"

said the girl. "The Practigard makers, they are our richest mennen."

But after a time, Practigards and similar matters gradually lost interest for Roy.

"Say, Verne, I'm sure in luck to have you show me all this," he said, stepping down from his high chair. "Believe me, I never guessed what—well, what nice girls they have on Mercury."

"I'm sure," she countered, smiling at him through the half-light, "on the planety Earth, the girls, they are much more nice."

"Oh, no! Why, not the finest of them—"

He paused, a little alarmed at his own boldness. But encouraged by a beaming look from beneath her flaxen curls, he went on, haltingly, "Judging from what I've seen, I'm going to be mighty sorry to go back to the Earth at all."

"Oh, but *must* you?" she flashed out.

He drew a bit nearer. And then, just as he was wondering how to put assurance enough into his reply, *it* happened.

At first he did not know where it came from, but it had the stertorous loudness of a foghorn. It was followed—or, rather, accompanied—by a screeching as of a fire alarm, a wailing as of an air-raid siren, the shrieking and screaming of factory whistles, and a clanging as of enormous bells.

Verne had turned pale. Her mouth gaped wide. She threw one agitated hand across her chest, while with the other she pointed at the loud-speaker on the wall, from which the commotion was proceeding.

"Come!" she gasped, in words that Roy surmised rather than heard amid the uproar. "Follow me!"

She darted out to the corridor, into which scores of people had poured from dozens of doors. Some were running to the left, some to the right. They pushed against one another, collided, fell over each other. Some carried babes in arms; others were followed by bawling children. A few clutched precious bags and bundles, only to drop them amid the excitement. The faces of all were drawn, blanched, haggard; many were crying out and babbling incoherently.

Suddenly the din of the bells, whistles, and sirens ceased. But it was followed immediately by a voice that spoke from loud-speakers throughout the building.

"Mennen and women, this is the Public Informationer! Be calm! Walk, but run not to your posts! Walk, but run not! You have heard only an alarm. There is no proof of danger yet. Let me repeat. *There is no proof of danger!*"

Far from soothing the crowd, these words seemed to increase the panic.

"What do you—what do you think?" Roy managed to blurt out as he and Verne turned a corner into another corridor filled with stampeding people.

He saw the disconsolate glance she threw him, the terror in her bright sea-blue eyes.

"Take not the Tubelators! Caution! Take not the Tubelators!" the Air Voice resumed, in a rumbling drone. "Should the power be shut off, they would be not safe! Walk! Walk, but run not!"

To Roy it was easy to spring along. Gravity was so much less than on Earth that he thought nothing of ten-foot leaps. But it was otherwise for the Mercurites, with their spindly legs and their lack of practice in walking. Many were panting and puffing. Some collapsed.

"Until the emergency is over, it is forbidden to use Practigards!" the Air Voice boomed on. "By order of the Bureaudent, it is forbidden, unless you are on Government servicing!"

Meanwhile the fugitives hastened through four or five corridors and descended several emergency flights of stairs, then passed through a high triangular doorway and out of an enormous apartment house, whose dark stone wall shot high above.

"The lights? What's happened to the lights?" Roy broke out.

No longer was the scene brilliant with bluish and milky white lamps, shining in triangles, rectangles, pentagons, and hexagons from the pavements and the branching roof supports. All was dark, except for occasional weaving firefly lights and the far-circling, many-hued searchlights that swept portions of the ceiling. Here and there, through the transparent dome, the stars could be seen.

Only now did Roy begin to feel the contagion of fear that convulsed the people swarming about him in the darkness.

"Be concerned not that the lights are off!" the Air Voice once more made itself heard. "Cause for worry, there is none! The lightifying system, it is intact! The lights, by order of the Bureaudent, they have been turned off, so that the source of the damage we may discover!"

"It's lucky Granner is in charge," Roy heard Verne's voice, as she pressed her mouth close to his ear. "With him at the head, we have not anything to fear."

Roy, as he framed a mental picture of the Bureaudent, did not feel quite so confident. But he whispered a hopeful word. More by instinct than by deliberate will, his hand reached down, found a small one at his side, and pressed it reassuringly.

"Now I take my post!" she whispered to him, in tones that he could barely make out. "I am one of the Searching Eyes."

Immediately she uncovered a small recess in the pavement and drew out what looked like a machine gun. This she pointed upward; then, standing back a few feet, she pulled a lever. Instantly a red rocket-like flare shot toward the Plastidome, but burst before reaching it, scattering brilliant white sparks. Time after time, she repeated this act, always aiming at a different part of the Plastidome.

"This is a photographer," she said, "to make pictures of the Plastidome. These pictures, we can develop them fast, and see if they show any hole or crack."

"Mennen and women, we repeat! Mennen and women, we repeat!" the Air Voice burst forth once more. "There is not any proof yet of danger! Not any proof at all!"

At this announcement, the murmurings and mutterings seemed to grow still louder.

Now, from the broad avenue before the building, bright new lights were darting. Vaguely Roy could make out a large Practigard, which, with gigantic leaps, was bounding between the great roof-supporting columns. From this Practigard new searchlight streamers swept the Plastidome with sharp white blades of light, which, after a time, were concentrated on one point.

"Maybe—maybe they have something found!" gasped Verne.

Then, from somewhere ahead, a tremendous clattering and crashing burst forth. And a new darkness descended as a cloud cut off large portions of the Plastidome.

"Yes, yes, they have something found!" Verne repeated. "They will seal it off! All will be well!"

But as the dismay of the people rose in an increasing roar, Roy thought that he knew how it felt to be a passenger on a sinking ship.

And what of Chris? How was Chris getting along in this emergency? Poor fellow! He had no Verne to stand by and reassure him.

It was hard to realize that, if the worst came to the worst, nobody on Earth would ever know what had happened to any of them. He and Chris would be considered lost on the way to Mercury; and not a soul on Earth would ever know about this marvelous Mercurite civilization. It would sink from sight without a trace—that is, unless new space-men did get here after a time and run across the ruins.

Then once more Roy was aware of the small figure at his side. And he hoped, he hoped more passionately than ever, that they would be saved.

Just then, during a pause in the commotion, he chanced to hear voices to his right.

"They say," remarked one man, "it was a big meteor. Right through the Plastidome it went!"

"Oh, no," dissented another, "it was a whole meteor shower! Many holes in the Plastidome it made! Our Bureaudent, he has ordered out all the reserves—"

An explosive sound, from somewhere in the open, cut short these words. There was a roar and a rumbling, and the cloud seemed to withdraw from parts of the Plastidome, revealing the stars where all had been opaque.

Then, from the multitude, a great cheer arose. "O-way! O-way! Way-o! Wheek! Wheek! Wheek!"

At the same instant, the lights went on.

"Mennen and women!" the Air Voice roared forth. "The emergency, it is over! The danger, by the skill of our Bureaudent, it is overcome! You may to your tasks return!"

But Roy thought he had never seen such a wan and wilted crowd as now began streaming back into the buildings.

CHAPTER IX

Chris lay full length on his bed, hands pillowing his head, while he listened to the Air Voice, which he switched to "Silence" as his roommate burst in.

"Ah, glad you're here!" Roy broke out. "Say, you missed it! There sure was one peach of an alarm!"

Chris lifted himself on one elbow and stared at his friend with a quizzical light in his electric-blue eyes. "You're telling *me?*"

"Oh! What do you know about it?"

Chris drew in his legs, and slowly arose. "More than you think. Believe me, more than anybody else on this whole darned planet."

Roy had crossed the room and seated himself on an undersized chair, his long legs stretched out before him. "Say, man, who do you think you're kidding?"

"I'm not kidding. It's the truth. Just sit there and

listen, boy. Got to promise, though, not to let on to any soul."

"I promise, so help me," agreed Roy, raising one hand with mock solemnity. "Now shoot!"

"Well," muttered Chris, taking a chair opposite Roy, "remember, I said I'd do a little exploring while you were away?"

Roy nodded.

"Right off, I began bumping into trouble. Found my way to the entrance of this building, and out into the street, which was crowded with Practigards. However, I thought I could slip around them. But I hadn't gone a dozen feet before I heard somebody shouting behind me, and turned to see a little guy in a green dress waving a dagger. 'Come back!' he yelled, in his crazy jargon. 'You can't there out go!'

" 'What's eating you?' I hollered at him, but might as well have spoken Greek. He came to me, looking real mad, and said, 'I am a Public Protectioner. You here are a stranger, so I will not to the Lockuppery take you this time. Do you know not you are law-breaking to walk on the street?'

" 'What you mean, law-breaking?' I bawled at him. He looked at me in a pitying sort of way, like he thought I was pretty dumb, and explained, 'Mennen that walk on the street, they with traffic interfere. The streets, they are for Practigards. If you want to use them, you must ride.'

" 'Okay,' I said, just to get rid of the guy. But what a crummy world, where a fellow can't take a walk without getting arrested! When he was gone, I said to myself, 'Well, suppose I do ride in a Practigard. Who the devil is going to stop me?' I saw about a dozen of them parked right at the entrance of the building. 'Maybe, if I try, I could run one,' I thought. 'Back on earth, I was a pretty good driver.' I opened the door of a little one, and peeked inside. There was a steering stick, and buttons of different colors, marked *'Start,' 'Stop,' 'Rise,' 'Descend,' 'Brakes,' 'Accelerate,' 'Decelerate,'* and so on. 'Looks simple enough,' I said to myself. 'Well, boy, nothing attempted, nothing done. Suppose you take a chance.' "

Roy let out a low whistle. "Take a chance? I'll say you did! Didn't you stop to consider there might be laws against Practigard-stealing?"

"Well, by gum, they wouldn't let me walk, so I figured I had a right to ride," Chris went on, with defiance in his voice, as he arose and began slowly pacing the room. "I got on all right, too, for a while. The damned thing was bumpy as a wild broncho. But the steering mechanism was mostly automatic, and simple enough for a low-grade moron. My problem was dodging those other Practigards, which came at me from above and below and on both sides. A dozen times I thought we'd collide. However, it was all mighty good sport."

"Couldn't anybody see you were a foreigner?"

"No, the driver's seat was enclosed with a clever sort of plastic, transparent from inside, but opaque from outside. I couldn't see the other drivers, and they couldn't see me."

"Even so, you don't realize what you might have run into. Weren't you afraid of getting lost?"

"No, I went down one street pretty nearly in a straight line—sort of a Mercurite Broadway. Only one thing really worried me. Suppose the damned contraption gave out of fuel? However, every now and then I saw other Practigards stopping before red posts that reminded me of fire signals. Each time, the driver got out and turned a little wheel near the top of the post. Then a nozzle would shoot out, and bury itself in a hole in the Practigard, where it stayed for a minute or two—anybody could see it was letting in fuel. I think they use some sort of concentrated fuel, much more powerful than gasoline."

Roy yawned. "Yes? Well, that's sure interesting. But what has it to do with that general alarm—"

"If you'll just pipe down, you'll find out!" snapped Chris. And then, irrelevantly, "Say, think they might have a cigarette anywhere on this planet?"

"If they did, man, you'd see me wreathed in smoke. But go on! I'm all keyed up about that alarm."

"Well," Chris resumed, "sure enough, I came face-to-face with the very thing I was scared of. I could feel the machine getting sort of fluttery about the heart. I looked around me for one of those red fuel poles, and just in the nick of time I noticed one a little way down a side street. However, it wasn't red,

but yellow, which I took to mean it gave out a different brand of fuel. There was just life enough left
in my Practigard to get to the yellow post before the
engine went dead."

"Yes, and maybe it didn't occur to you what a hell
of a risk you were taking, getting that stuff without
paying for it."

"Who said I'd get it without paying? I have Mercurite money, haven't I?" argued Chris, rattling two
or three little red and green plastic ellipses and hexagons. "Thought there might be a slot to slip the coins
into. Still, I was taking no chances. I waited till nobody was in sight, then quicker'n a flash I reached up
to a wheel on the yellow post. It was bigger than
those on the other posts, and stiffer'n sheet rock. But I
gave it a good hard yank, and then—heavens, things
started hopping!"

"Well, did it pour out your fuel?"

"Poured out a darned sight more than fuel!" Chris
took a quick turn about the room, and spoke with a
snort. "Let out the biggest hullabaloo you ever heard
—like all the bells, whistles, and sirens in the world
making a racket all at once. Right away, people began crowding out of doors, running in all directions
like headless hens. Practigards came bumping down
everywhere, and the drivers got out and ran. 'Funny,'
I thought, 'people aren't supposed to walk on the
streets, and now everybody's running on them.'

"I could see how scared those poor devils were,
and thought, 'Guess I ran a fire alarm by mistake.'

Luckily, nobody saw me, and besides, everybody was too frightened to notice. A minute later, all the lights went off. Say, did that give me an eerie feeling! But there was just light enough coming down through the Plastidome for me to see my way, and I beat it back right in the middle of those screaming, racing mobs—made a beeline for this room. Lord! I hope they don't find out!"

"If they do, man, they'll have your head. Especially, considering your red hair."

"My red hair?" demanded Chris, coming forward with a leap. "See here, have you gone plumb daffy?"

Roy shook his head. "Wish it was that simple, old fellow. But I've been wanting to tell you, and haven't known exactly how. However, you'd find out anyhow—might as well have it first from me—"

"Have *what* first from you?" Chris halted, and brought down two challenging fists. "What in blazes! Have they accused me of burglary—or murder?"

"No, but they've got—well, the damnedest prejudice against folks with red hair. They call them *Koskuffs,* which is almost a dirty word. That's why, if you've noticed—"

"Sure, I've noticed everyone's treated me like a stepchild. I couldn't figure out why they always gave me the neat bypass. But red hair? Lord! What do they want me to do? Dye mine flaxen? Say, old sport, wouldn't I look pretty, blossoming out as a platinum blonde?"

"With red showing at the roots!" gibed Roy. "But

it's too late to change, now that they've all seen the red."

"Well, this only bears out what I've been saying," meditated Chris, as he paused by the window and stared out at the Practigards hopping half a dozen stories below. "Remember, I had a hunch about this blasted place. Now we'd better beat it out just as fast as we can."

"Don't see how we possibly can, old man, till they let us. Besides, we've still got lots to learn here," objected Roy, who was framing visions of a bright-eyed face. "Say, what about hearing the Air Voice?"

He turned the switch to "Sound," and both men listened, fascinated.

". . . the Bureaudent, he has three committees appointed to investigate. The theories as to the unprecedentified alarm, they are very varied. A high government authority, who by name refuses to be mentioned, he says it was not anything at all, only a short circuit in the fuse box of the signalifying system. But another high official, in whose word this station the utmost reliance places, he has in private said to our Circulator that the alarm, it points to serious defects in our world defenses. Meanwhile, reports continue that the Plastidome, it has in several places been pierced. The Head Planicrat, he is quoted as saying that scientitioners, they are inspectoring the break. The people, they repeat the old saying: where there is moisture, there is water. . . ."

"Whew!" broke in Chris. "I sure never imagined what I was letting loose. Anyway, I'm safe so long as they don't suspect who did it."

". . . the world alarm and defense system, it will be an issue in the coming campaign," the Air Voice rambled on. "Pee-tere Will-lems, Chief Secretary of the Mennen's Dissident Party, he has accusified the Bureaustration of being asleep at the Plastidome. Anner-belle Strong, Chief Secretary of the Women's Dissident Party, she has a statement made that the trouble, it springs from the fault of the Bureaustration in putting not women enough in office. Both parties say that, in the electioning for new Planicrats, the question before the votifiers, it will be better world alarms and Plastidome protectioning. The motto of her party, says Miss Strong, will be 'Mother and home and the Plastidome!' . . ."

"Say, this is the first I knew of parties and elections down here," reflected Chris. "Maybe I'll run myself, on a platform 'Equal rights for redheads'—what the devil!"

Something that sounded like an organ peal had burst into music at the door. While the two men stood staring, the peal was repeated, louder and deeper. Only after the third peal did Roy grasp the idea. "Why, the doorbell!"

Two little men stood outside, half buried beneath mounds of clothing.

"The Head Planicrat, he asked us these to bring,"

explained one of the men, entering and throwing down his burden. "He has said you are to dress in civilizated clothes."

"What I'd like would be a razor," remarked Roy, running one hand over the facial growth of seven weeks. "But what's that there?"

He picked up a little instrument not too unlike the electric shaver he had used on Earth, and saw that there was also a pair of shears.

"If these clothes, they fit you not right, we give you others," said one of the men, who went down on his right knee, waved his right hand, and withdrew.

"When you're in Mercury, do as the Mercurites do," decided Roy, as he looked glumly over the six or eight tunics and the rubbery-looking sandals. "Which do you think you'd prefer, old fellow? That cherry-red outfit? Or maybe that sky-blue one?"

"And you, old man," Chris took up, "I can't quite figure out whether this lemon-yellow affair would be most becoming on you, or that dainty pink dress."

"Lordy! Am I glad Mom can't see her little boy now!" muttered Roy, when he had adjusted the only tunic that seemed halfway to fit him: a peacock-green garment, with saffron trimmings. And Chris, who had no choice but a lavender tunic with vermilion dots and stripes, made a wry face as he stared down at his knees and well-developed calves, now fully exposed.

"Well, if we cut a few of these bushes off our faces,

we'll look halfway human again," Roy decided,
wielding the shears. "Want to lend me your face to
start on, old man?"

As he set to work, he could again hear the Air
Voice. "The Bureaudent, he assures the people there
is nothing wrong with the Plastidome. Positively
nothing wrong. Our world defenses, they are as
sound as ever. . . ."

CHAPTER X

As another long, deep organ blast sounded at the door, the two men started up in surprise.

"Wonder if it's those same clothes men again?" asked Roy. "Maybe they want to see how your dress fits, old fellow."

But when the door opened, all that he saw was a small, frightened-looking man dangling a thread about a yard long.

"Message for Mr. Roy King!"

"Okay! Where is it?"

The man held out the blue thread.

"Yes, but where's the message?"

"The message, it is here," stated the newcomer, still holding out the thread. And then, indulgently, as to a child, "You take this—put it on your string recordifier—"

"What makes you think I've got a string record-ifier?"

"All mennen, they have string recordifiers. It is law-required. Here! If you will permit, I will show!"

Roy nodded, and the man entered, and pressed a little black button near the door. Instantly a wall panel rattled open, and a "string recordifier," no bigger than a man's hand, shot into view.

"You put the string on here. See!" instructed the visitor, attaching the blue thread to a small knob on one reel of the recorder. "When you want to hear the message, you press that yellow button. To make your reply, you press the green button."

"Oh, so I'm expected to reply?"

"Naturally. On the same string. Speak loud and clear. This will take a two-minute message. Now I go into the hall. When the message, it is ready, you open the door and call me."

"Whew! Sounds like a neat little system!" commented Chris, bending over the machine curiously. "Well, wonder what sweet little Juliet is sending notes to her Romeo?"

"Most likely," conjectured Roy, "it's something that old duck the Bureaudent forgot to tell me. Well, we'll find out!"

He pressed the yellow button. Instantly there was a whirring and rumbling, lasting five or ten seconds. Then, low and clear and wonderfully soft, a feminine voice was heard.

"Roy King! Greetings from the Octagon Branch of the Women's Concurrent Party! This is Verne Wyle, Chairodent. The other members, they like to know what a man from the planety Earth thinks about our world's alarm system. If you can a few words say to us, take Tubelator Nineteen at twenty-five per cent past the twenty-first hour. Answer by this string."

Another whirr and rumbling, and the machine was still.

Chris had crossed the room almost at a leap, and was clapping Roy resoundingly on the shoulder. "Congratulations, old man! You're sure making the grade. Verne Wyle—isn't she that swell-looker? Come, come now, don't get so red in the face. If you're scared to accept the invitation, I'll always pinch-hit for a pal."

"I'll take you along, old fellow—but no, I can't," decided Roy, remembering Chris's red hair. "Twenty-five per cent past the twenty-first hour— that must be about three fifteen P.M."

Having pressed the green button, Roy spoke his reply, and after giving the thread back to the messenger, he stood looking out of the window, as if the sight of the Practigards hopping below was of sudden enormous interest.

"Better hurry!" Chris gibed. "It's, well—let's see —about fifty per cent past the fifteenth hour already. You've only got about five hours and three quarters. However, don't forget; my offer to pinch-hit still holds good."

Roy had wheeled about for a scathing retort, when once more they heard that organ-like sound.

"For the love of Pete!" exclaimed Chris, letting out a low whistle. "Say, we're getting to be more popular than the winners in a beauty contest."

He pulled the door open, and stared into the face of the Planicrat, who was accompanied by two other bald-headed, elderly men, each of whom carried a little green case.

The official thrust his way past Chris without seeming to see him. But he made the usual formal bows before Roy.

"Mr. Roy King," said the Planicrat, "these two mennen, they are Dr. Eddi-ward Robb and Dr. Rich-hard Cross. They are expert Word Chiselfiers. I myself have used them for my books. They will your story hear about the planety Earth, and then will your book write."

The "Word Chiselfiers" had opened their little green cases, from which they drew several string recorders—or rather, super-recorders, for each held half a dozen reels of blue string, and each was as large as a fair-sized book.

"These machines, they will take down a story ten hours long," explained Eddi-ward Robb, wiring the instruments together. "Can we begin?"

Roy nodded, and the Planicrat, with elaborate gestures of respect, withdrew. Meanwhile the other visitors, not appearing to notice Chris, had taken seats.

"Now," began Dr. Rich-hard Cross, after pressing a button that caused all six reels of one of the

machines to start revolving, "remember that we
know no more of the Earth's last five hundred years
than of the next five hundred. So like ignorant children we must our questions ask. What would you say
was the most important thing about the planety
Earth in these five centuries?"

Roy pondered, but in vain.

"I'd say," answered Chris, though the visitors still
appeared unaware of his existence, "the most important thing is that we haven't fought any more wars."

Dr. Robb shuddered slightly. Dr. Cross's brow was
furrowed with a frown. But the string recorder,
which had no prejudices, reeled on and on, taking
down Chris's words.

"I'd say the next most important thing," Chris
continued, "was that the people, after the lesson of
the Hydrogen Death, began working together, and
formed a world government, which has ruled ever
since, enabling many countries to get back on their
feet."

Dr. Robb and Dr. Cross cocked their heads.

"The third most important thing," Chris went
on, "is that their old worship of wealth was gone.
They came to realize that what counted was not what
a man had, but what he was. Since rich men hadn't
been able to keep the world from being blown to
smithereens, the people began for a change to give
the man of brains a chance. All our great leaders, for
these five hundred years, have been scholars, scien-
tists, and literary men."

Still the reels of the recorder went round and round.

"What's your world like today?" Dr. Cross asked Roy.

"Just like Chris has said."

"There are still millions of square miles where no one has ever lived since the Hydrogen Death," said Chris. "But gradually our people are spreading out again, clearing the wasteland where great cities used to be."

"What were some of those cities?" Dr. Robb asked Roy.

"Let's see," answered Roy. "Well, there were places called Paris and Berlin. And another called Mos—Mos something."

"And New York. And Rome. And Sydney. And Buenos Aires. And Athens," amended Chris. "Of late a few pioneers have been struggling to the wilderness that used to be western Europe, and the eastern part of a country called—what was it—oh, yes, the United States."

The reels of the recorder still revolved.

"The place of science—what now is it on the planety Earth?" asked Dr. Cross, with a stealthy sidelong glance at Chris. "Science—it caused the Hydrogen Death. Maybe the people, they like it not any more."

"Science wasn't what caused the Hydrogen Death," Chris denied. "It was the way people thought and acted about science. You don't blame dynamite, do you, if some imbecile explodes it? We now realize we've got to keep science from the imbeciles. It's high explosive—not everybody ought to handle it. So we've set up an International Science Commission, which passes on all new inventions, and only permits development of those the world is ready for."

"It is the same on Mercury," said Dr. Robb. "To use inventions the world is unready for—that would be like letting children drive Practigards."

And so the talk went on and on. The questions continued to be put to Roy, but were all answered by Chris, who had done much reading in the history of the post-Hydrogen era. It was almost the twenty-first hour when the session ended. But the "Word Chiselfiers" would not leave without an appointment to return next morning at the fifteenth hour.

As they took up their green cases and shuffled out, they both had the sleek, contented looks of cats who have found the bird-hunting good.

"I've just time for that appointment," said Roy, as he prepared for a cool plunge into the Sprayeleter. Chris meanwhile was helping himself to some tidbits, which had come to him in a pneumatic tube after he had pressed a button marked *"Mid-Break."*

But Roy was too excited to eat. "See you in a few hours, old chap," he said, as he burst out of the room. "And say, don't ring any more general alarms while I'm gone!"

Feeling just a little glum, Chris drifted over to the window and glanced out at the Practigards leaping

and hopping along the street. He noticed in particu-
lar a snow-white one, with dome-shaped blue markings; occasionally it let out a blast like thunder,
while the others made way before it.

"What the devil's a fellow to do now?" he pondered. "Maybe I could risk it again and drive one of
those darned machines."

However, what would he do this time if the power
gave out? He was still muddling over this problem
when he was again startled by that long, deep organ
sound at the door, and opened it to face a youth of
about twenty, who stood there dangling a blue
thread.

"Message for Room E119!"

"Okay! Which of us is it for?"

The young man looked up at the red-haired stranger, and shrank back, shuddering.

"Nobody said. They only gave the room number."

"Well then, maybe it's for me. You wait here
while I try it on the string recorder."

"String recordifier."

A minute later, Chris was listening to the message:

"Greetings! This is Elva Lanne, First Secretary,
Rhomboid Branch, Women's Dissident Party. Today
we have an assemblifying to discuss the world's
alarm system. We like much to be honored by the
man from the planety Earth, if he will to us a few
words speak. Come just as soon as you can. Take
Tubelator Twenty. Answer by the string."

"Could mean me," Chris thought, though he well knew that it did not mean him. "Anyway, Roy can't be in two places at once. And it'll give me something to pass the time."

Without hesitation, he answered. "Your invitation received. Will be there right away."

"Say, wait a minute!" he called, as the messenger started off with the blue thread. "Can you tell me what the Women's Dissident Party is?"

The young man came a step nearer, but still kept a good distance between himself and the formidable-looking stranger.

"The Women's Dissident Party, it is the party that is not the Women's Concurrent Party."

"But what's the difference? What do they stand for?"

The messenger's clear, innocent face had a puzzled look. "I've never heard anyone say," he answered, shaking his head.

"Why do they call them the *Women's* Dissident and the *Women's* Concurrent Party? Do the women have their own parties?"

"Of course. How could you have women and mennen in the same party?"

"Why not? We do down on Earth, you know."

The youth's eyes widened with wonder.

"What a funny planety!" he marveled. "I've always heard it said you could let not women vote for mennen, or mennen for women, because they would decide not for the best candidate, but for the one with the most sex attractioning."

"Oh! Well, that *is* an idea!" laughed Chris. "How do you arrange it then, having your men—I mean, your mennen—and your women in separate parties?"

The youth looked more puzzled than ever.

"I know not what you mean. The women, they elect their own officers. The mennen, they elect theirs. You will see when we vote for our new Planicrats. The Head Planicrat, he is elected by the mennen's parties. The Women's Planicrat, she is elected by the women's parties."

"How do you manage, having two of the same officer?"

"But what is hard about that? The Head Planicrat, it is an old custom, he marries the Women's Planicrat."

"Well, that sure is nice—that is, if they pick a sweet, charming Women's Planicrat. But suppose he —or she—is married already?"

"I understand not," answered the youth, trying hard to cope with the strange ideas of a strange world. "On the planety Earth, does no one ever marry to better himself in life? It is all so simple. The candidates' State duties, they come first. Therefore, by an old law, their old marriage, it is said to be no marriage at all. If they like not this law, they go not into politicking."

"Whew! I always said politics was a queer game," mused Chris, while the young man, dangling the blue thread, mumbled a parting syllable and dashed off down the corridor.

"Might as well find Tubelator Twenty," Chris told himself. And though he could never get used to the idea of being shot in a coffin-sized container through a pneumatic tube, he resigned himself with an oath, since he knew of no other way to reach the meeting place.

As he got out of Tubelator Twenty, he found himself in a long gallery before a lighted O-shaped open doorway, which led to an anteroom, where an amiable-looking dark-haired young woman sat at a desk. To her rear was another doorway, permitting glimpses of rows of chairs more than half filled with women.

The girl at the desk seemed surprised to see him, but there was a pleasant smile on her olive-shaped face.

"I'm Chris Hartridge," he introduced himself. "I've come on your invitation."

"I am Elva Lanne, First Secretary of this Branch," she said, seeming just a little flustered as she glanced doubtfully about her. "Our Chairodent—oh, I don't know—I'm afraid there must be a little mistaking," she gasped, in an incoherent way. "You go right on in, and take a seat. To our Chairodent I will speak as soon as I can."

The lovely violet-blue eyes, beneath the long

black lashes, looked up, Chris thought, with the first friendliness he had yet seen in any Mercurite.

He was still thinking of those eyes when he stepped into the meeting place—a large hall where a hundred and fifty or two hundred women were seated on rows of tiny chairs, while a fat old crone, with a sharp chin outthrust above double chins, stood on the platform in a violet tunic, haranguing with heated gesticulations of her tiny arms.

Chris sat down in a rear row, on a chair much too small for him. His legs, he thought, had never before been so cramped. The next row, besides, was so close that it hardly left room for his knees. But that, of course, was because the Mercurites were so much smaller than Earth-people.

As his gaze traveled to the platform and he noticed the woman seated beside the speaker, a chill ran through him. Staring down at him with a dutchess-like contempt, was the blade-like face, the long protruding nose, the angular chin, and the hawk eyes of Marigold Har-reys.

"Heavens!" he thought. "If I'd only known!"

He had an idea of slipping quietly out—especially as he saw the women on nearby chairs edging gradually away, leaving a wide space between him and them. But he thought of that nice violet-eyed girl in the anteroom, and decided to stay.

CHAPTER XI

". . . Yes, women of the Dissident Party, she is one of our most distinguishified members. No woman Circulator on Mercury has a more honorific record. As our party's candidate for the high office of Women's Planicrat, she would great justice do us. Therefore I say we should nominify our good and beloved leader, our Chairodent, Miss Marigold Har-reys."

The old dame in the violet tunic bowed and took her seat, and a tumult of applause broke forth. "O-way! O-way! Way-o! Wheek! Wheek! Wheek!" Chris was surprised that such small women could make such a tremendous noise.

Smiling, Marigold took the floor. "Miss Ell-ey-yott, I much thank you," she began. "Great pleasure it gives me to be so honored by a woman like you, a most distinguishified member of the Dissident Party, and Chairodent of that great organizationing, the Daughters of the Plastidome."

"Wheek! Wheek! Wheek! O-way! O-way! Way-o!"
rang out the applause.

Chris found it hard to follow Marigold's next
words, which were spoken with rapid-fire delivery in
a rasping voice. But he did gather, that if it were her
duty for the sake of the party and the planet to run
for Women's Planicrat, she would not be found un-
willing to make the sacrifice.

"O-way! O-way! Way-o! Wheek! Wheek! Wheek!"
the appluase roared forth again. And Chris thought
pityingly of the candidate for Head Planicrat, who,
if he and she were both elected, would have to marry
Marigold.

"Now for the topic of the day," said Marigold,
after the cheering had died down. "This concerns
the bad world defenses made by the Concurrent
Party, as we all from the recent disgraceous alarm
could see."

She paused, and Chris felt the withering glance of
her hawk's eyes. But just then, from the anteroom,
the dark-eyed girl burst forward. "Oh, Miss Chairodent," Chris heard her break out, "before you anything else say, there is something I must to you
speak." And for several minutes the two women en-
gaged in an earnest conference.

It may have been that they let their voices ring out
louder than they realized. Or maybe Mercurite
ears were less acute than those of Earth people, so
that the speakers did not suspect that Chris could
make out what they were saying.

"No, no, no, Miss Lanne, it is not possible," Marigold protested in a squeak, while she still fixed a hard glance in Chris's direction. "I meant the other man. When I told you to message him, I knew not the two were in the same room living."

Chris missed the next words. And then, softer and gentler, he heard Miss Lanne's protest: "But you asked him. Besides, I myself—I see nothing wrong with Koskuffs. It is all foolishness, an old prejudice—"

Chris could not quite make out Marigold's reply, though he could hear the shrill, grating tones. But he was not interested in what she said; his discomfort was too great. With his knees hunched up before him in that cramping attitude, his legs were going to sleep; he wanted very much to slip away. However, he could not leave that nice Miss Lanne in the lurch.

Then his eyes strayed to a spot halfway down the aisle, and he wondered why he had been so blind. Here was just the place for him! Between two of the chairs of the row ahead, there was an open space just large enough for his feet. No, not exactly an open space; two dull strips of metal, shaped like the foot pedals of a piano, projected about six inches above the floor, amid a little fence of meshed wire. What were they for? Obviously, as footstools for long legs like his.

Congratulating himself on the discovery, Chris moved to the seat behind the footrests. And then, while Marigold's voice came to him in a particularly bitter rasp—"But we simply can't, the party members would never forgive us!"—Chris stretched out his long legs.

He was as much startled as anyone at the immediate uproar of applause. "O-way! O-way! Way-o! Wheek! Wheek! Wheek!" The commotion was, if anything, louder than before. But as he glanced about him, he saw that none of the women were cheering. All were staring at him with gaping mouths and gasps of horror. One or two were motioning distractedly. But the applause went on.

Then, as a terrible suspicion flashed over him, he lifted one foot from the metallic rest. The applause continued, but at half its previous volume. He removed both feet, and the applause ended. But when he put his left foot experimentally back on the strips of metal, there was a renewed outburst of "O-way! Wheek! Wheek!" And as his glance flashed to the ceiling, he noticed the loud-speakers—and understood everything. "String recordifiers," evidently, had many uses.

Dagger-like was the long, thin finger of Marigold Har-reys as it pointed at him accusingly. And dagger-like was her strident, accusing voice. "Koskuff! Koskuff!"

"Koskuff! Koskuff! Koskuff!" several of the women echoed, with angry cries. "Koskuff! Koskuff! Koskuff!"

Agitated figures were springing from their seats; wrathful eyes darted fire at him. Everyone, apparently, thought that he had started the applause-machine deliberately.

He, too, had shot to his feet. But as he opened his mouth to explain, an increasing chorus of fury drowned his words. "Koskuff! Koskuff! Go away, Koskuff! Go away!"

He had a glimpse of Miss Lanne on the platform, pleading with Marigold. But the chorus of "Koskuff! Koskuff! Go away, Koskuff!" was like a rising gale. And in a raging wave the women were bearing down upon Chris.

"Good Lord," he thought, "if I don't beat a quick retreat, they'll tear me like wolves!"

With a leap, he cleared two rows of chairs. His last glance, as he bolted out of the door, showed him Marigold still on the platform, her face an apoplectic red as she swung one arm irately in his direction.

Feeling considerably flustered, he did not take the Tubelator back to his room, but wandered for two hours through the endless corridors of the buildings before at last a passing messenger guided him aright.

"Whew!" he reflected. "Never thought the day would come when Chris Hartridge would be routed by a bunch of clubwomen. But Samson himself couldn't stand up against that gang."

Nevertheless, the picture that kept coming back to him was not of the hateful Miss Har-reys but of the lovely Miss Lanne.

When he slouched back into his room, he found

Roy already stalking about, elation on his face. "Say, I just got back. Where've you been? Getting into more trouble?"

"Believe me I have! What's happened to you? Still making a hit with the dames?" tossed out Chris, as he wearily stretched himself out on his bed.

"Oh, I wouldn't say that," Roy denied, with a nonchalant gesture. "Truth is, however, they did ask me to speak more than once. Everybody was awfully nice. I was a little surprised at the amount of the applause."

"Applause?" Chris caught up, throwing his head back and breaking into a roar. "By gum, I'll bet you got an earful!"

Roy stared questioningly at his friend. "What's so funny, if they did applaud me?"

The word "applaud" was enough to send Chris off into new spasms. "Well—and after the applause, did they ask you to visit them some more?"

"Fact is, they did," acknowledged Roy, a telltale blush overspreading his face. "She—that is, they, asked me to speak at another meeting, day after to-morrow. Now let's hear just what you were up to?"

"First let me get my breath back. Here, let's have a bite," proposed Chris, springing off the bed and pressing a button marked *"Evening Break."* "Also, how about tuning in on the Air Voice?"

He turned the switch, and listened, while he and Roy swallowed their food without half tasting it.

". . . the sides, they are forming for the coming

electioning for Planicrats. The Mennen's Concurrent Party, they are said much trouble to be having picking a candidate, since the present Head Planicrat, who the legal age has passed, he can run not again. The Women's Dissident Party, if the rumorings can be believed, it is planning to nominify that most eminent Circulator, well known to all readers of the *Purple Sheet,* Miss Marigold Har-reys—"

"The devil!" Chris broke in. "Do I have to hear that old crow's name whereever I go?"

"What's the matter, old chap?" demanded Roy, with a quizzical smile. "Has the sweet lady turned down your advances?"

But just then the Air Voice broke out in booming tones: "Special! News Item!"

A moment's silence followed, while Roy paused in the act of lifting a morsel of mock-bread to his mouth.

"We have just learned that a riot, it flamed forth this afternoon at the Rhomboid Branch of the Women's Dissident Party. Our Circulator, he has found that the disturbancy was caused by the Koskuff from the planety Earth, who broke into the meeting to make trouble. When nobody was looking, he stamped down on the applause footgear, making a great commotioning. As everybody knows, this is law-breaking. The women at the meeting, most indignant they were. But the Koskuff, he threatened them, and would much harm have done except for the courageousness of Chairodent Marigold Har-reys, who had the culprit seized and thrown out . . ."

"What a damned pack of lies!" Chris broke out, springing up and shaking his fist as if he would have liked to throttle someone. "Don't believe a word of it, Roy! If I could get hold of the fraud who concocted that yarn—"

"Anyway, sure looks like you started something," decided Roy, while his companion paced the floor with fists still clenched and shaking. "What's the matter, old fellow? Can't I even trust you out of sight?"

". . . the expulsion order against Miss Elva Lanne," the Air Voice went on, "it was confirmed by Chairodent Har-reys, who asserts that Miss Lanne, she an un-Mercurian act committed by defending a Koskuff. The vote, expelling Miss Lanne from the Rhomboid Branch, it was unanimous. Miss Har-reys says that the circumstances, they were most aggravifying. It much hurt her to move against Miss Lanne, but she had not any choice."

"Lord, that's awful!" groaned Chris. "Who would ever have expected that, just for saying a decent word—" He broke off, took another stride about the room, savagely shut off the Air Voice, which had turned to another subject, and bewailed, "The worst of it is, I don't even know where she is— can't get a word to her, to say how sorry I am."

"Never expected it of you, Chris," gibed Roy, "that you'd hardly be here a day before you'd get a

girl into disgrace. Now maybe you'll tell me just
what the mess is all about?"

"Wish I could figure it out myself," mused Chris.
"This Elva—say, I'd sure like to meet her twin sister back home. It all started just after you left this
afternoon and that doorbell rang—I'll be darned!
There she goes again!"

This time a messenger, standing in the corridor,
dangled not one blue thread, but four.

"Messages for Mr. Hartridge!"

"What, all for me?" shouted Chris. "Holy mack-
erel! I'm getting to be so popular you won't be able
to see me through the blushes." And then, to the
messenger, "Better wait out here till I see if there's
any reply."

"Well, you've got me beat, all right," Roy mur-
mured, admiringly. "Thought I did well to get one
at a time."

Chris meanwhile was drawing the "string recordifier" out of its niche and attaching one of the blue
threads. "Can't imagine who can want me," he muttered. "Well, let's hear the worst!"

"To Chris Hartridge, greetings!" a voice rang
out. "I am Frank Will-eys, Chairodent of the Mercurite Protectioning League. We are obliged to tell
you that Koskuffs, on this planety they are wanted
not. We are horrified and amazified to learn of your
thuggery at the Women's Dissident Party. Therefore, as good citizens of Mercury, we ask you to go
back fast where you came from."

"Well, sure looks like I've been making myself well liked," remarked Chris. "Now let's hear the next love note."

"To Christopher Hartridge, greetings!" the communication began, in the usual formal style. "I am Eye-leen Ell-ey-yott, Chairodent of the World Society of Daughters of the Plastidome. As a spokeswoman for the wives and mothers of the world, I protestify your brutal invasioning of women's rights. I shall with the authorities confer and see that they the proper punishing will inflict. Yours for a hundred per cent pure planety. Mercury for the Mercurites!"

"Wow!" Chris broke out, mopping his brow. "Wonder what she means by proper punishing?"

Automatically he took up the third thread.

"To Christopher Hartridge, greetings!" came the message, in a masculine voice. "I am your Bureaudent. I have with the most grave concern heard of your outrage at the Women's Dissident Party. Knowing that you are only a foreigner, I will send you not to the Lockuppery, as my advisors ask. But I see that it is not safe for a Koskuff to go out alone. Therefore this I order: henceforth you must be seen not outside your room except with your friend from the planety Earth or some citizen of Mercury. Otherwise, to the Lockuppery you go!"

"Good Lord!" Chris thundered. "Must I have a guardian like a two-year-old?"

"Sure looks that way," groaned Roy, appearing

troubled. "Worst of all, it seems like the guardian will have to be this poor goat here."

"Well, believe me, I sympathize with you, old fellow. You sure don't want me sticking my neck into your nice tête-a-têtes with *her*. Only way out, as I've said, is via a hurry trip back to Earth."

"Not yet—heavens, not yet!" protested Roy, while Chris absently ranged about the room. "Say, are you forgetting? There's still another blue thread."

"Yes, might as well hear who else is taking a whack at me," conceded Chris, as he snatched up the fourth thread.

But this time the voice was low and sweet-sounding, with none at all of the stridency of the other messages.

"Greetings to Christopher Hartridge! Maybe you remember me not. I am the girl who spoke to you in the anteroom of the Women's Dissident Party. I have much grief at the way my people treat you. You deserve it not. So I must my apologizings make for the other women. They know not any better. I am stricken to the heart. I wish I could know that you forgave us."

CHAPTER XII

"Now there's the right kind of girl! She sure deserves a good answer!" cried Chris, hopping up and down with such enthusiasm that you would never have guessed he had been in the pit of depression a moment before. "I take back what I was just thinking about every Mercurite."

"But say, boy, *who* is this Elva?" demanded Roy. "Maybe you'll introduce me?"

Chris, not seeming to hear these words, was already slipping the string back into the recorder.

"This is Chris Hartridge," he said, after pressing the button marked *Reverse*. "Your message made me very happy. I'd like to thank you in person, and tell you how sorry I am they threw you out of the Dissident Party, all on account of me. Unluckily, I don't know where to find you, and the Bureaudent has ordered me locked up in my room unless I go out with a companion. . . ."

The message ended only when, after two minutes, Chris had reached the end of the blue thread. Then, throwing open the door, he called to the messenger. "Take this at once to Miss Elva Lanne. Know her address?"

The messenger nodded, and was gone.

It was not more than half an hour before the same organ-like notes sounded again at the door and Chris received another blue thread. Roy noticed that his fingers were slightly unsteady as he adjusted the thread on the recorder.

"Greetings to Chris Hartridge!" the message vibrated in clear, soft feminine tones. "I thank you, my friend, for your kind words. But great distress it gives me to learn that the Bureaudent, in your room he has ordered you to stay unless you have a companion. I—though I am nobody at all—would like to make up to you for some of the things you have suffered. If you think it not a great presuming on my part, I would like to companionfy you so that you may see the different parts of the world. I am in Quarters XC 1178, which is reached by Tubelator Nine. Please answer by the same string."

"Lord! You're sure hitting things up fast!" burst out Roy.

Chris glared at him. "*You* ought to be glad she'll take me off your hands, old man," he retorted pointedly. "Let's see, what's a good time to go to her? Tomorrow at the fifteenth hour?"

"Why such a rush? Those Word Chiselers will be

here then," Roy reminded his friend, appealingly.

"Oh, all right, old chap, I won't let you down," Chris agreed, just a little reluctantly. "Then I'd better put things off, say, to about the twentieth hour. You'll go with me as far as her place, won't you —just so I'm not picked up and sent to the lockup?"

Roy nodded, while Chris put the thread back on the recorder, to hear Elva's words all over again.

The next day's session with the "Word Chisel-fiers" was a repetition of the previous interview; all the questions were put to Roy, and Chris did most of the answering. At the end of the meeting, which lasted four hours, Doctors Robb and Cross again smiled as if in great secret satisfaction, and left with laden record threads, after arranging to come again next day. "In four or five days more," said Robb, bowing deferentially to Roy as he left, "we will have all the informationing we need, and your book, it will then be written."

"He means, *your* book, Chris," said Roy, as the door closed upon their visitors. But Chris was busily consulting his wrist watch. "Say, old fellow," he asked, "about how much before the twentieth hour do you think we should set out?"

Forty minutes later, Roy left him before a door marked XC 1178. "Well, have a good time! When do you want me to call for you?" he asked. "In a couple of hours?"

"No—better make it three or four."

The next minute, Chris had pulled at a little steel panel before the door, and a beaming young woman had answered the organ-like summons.

He observed her now more closely than before, and could not decide whether he was most attracted by her lovely face or by something that shone behind the face. Her olive-shaped countenance showed regular, well-formed features; her straight hair, as dark as black coffee, had been combed all about her shapely head down to the shoulders, in the local style; her violet-blue eyes looked out as with a twinkling of small lights. But what he noticed most of all was the warmth, the sympathy that spoke from her wide, rippling smile, as from her soft, rich voice.

"Ah, Mr. Hartridge! I am glad you are here," she said, as she led him in.

He was surprised to find himself in a sort of laboratory. All about the large room, he saw "string recordifiers"—small ones and big, two-reeled and many-reeled, wired to batteries and to plugs in the walls, some with blue spools of thread, and some with orange, purple, yellow, and tomato red. On one side there was a table covered with pliers, screwdrivers, and other tools; dozens of jars and vials, on shelves against the wall, were evidently filled with chemical reagents.

"I hope you will your pardon grant," she said, with conventional politeness, "for asking you to my shop."

"*My* pardon? I ought to pour out my thanks," he answered as he stared curiously at a machine resembling an oversized microscope. "But I must say I'm surprised. What is this shop of yours?"

Her cheeks, which had not quite the waxen pallor of most of her countrymen, were touched by a passing rose hue.

"Oh, it is only a small shop," she deprecated, with a shrug. "My living, I make it repairing string recordifiers."

"Good! As an Earthman, that interests me. On our planet, we don't let women do much repair work."

"Why not?" she asked, turning upon him the full glow of her round, innocent eyes. "In delicate work, like fixing tiny recordifiers, we are told that women, with their smaller hands, they are better than mennen. I used with the Man-Multipliers to work, but they were much more hard."

"Man what?" he asked, supposing this to be some local form of calculating machine. But his attention quickly turned to other matters.

"Say, I don't want to butt in on you," he went on, as he moved slowly about the room, absently fingering some plastic reels no larger than his thumbnail.

"Go right on with your work."

"Butt in? What means that?" she asked. And when he had explained, she answered, "Oh, but you butt not in. I wanted much to see you and tell you how angry I am with my people for the cruel way they treated you. I want to help compensatify you for the wrong they've done you."

"What about the wrong they've done *you*, Miss—"

"Call me Elva."

"And call me Chris. I wish I knew some way to make up for what your party's done to you, Elva. Say! I've got it! Maybe I can help out in fixing those recorders—I mean, recordifiers."

"Maybe so, Chris. Maybe great knowledge you bring from the planety Earth. Maybe some great discovery you give us—and then the people, they forget that you are a Koskuff."

"Well, maybe—but I can't believe it," decided Chris, as he still went about inspecting strings, wires, and wheeled mechanisms. "You know, I always did like fixing things. Ever since I was six, and took my mother's alarm clock apart. So if you'll help me get on to the hang of things—"

"Oh, good!" she approved, clapping her hands with joy. "I am the most luckiest girl on Mercury to have a man from the planety Earth help me!"

As he saw the lights sparkling in those bright violet-blue eyes, it was hard for him to keep his mind on "string recordifiers."

Her first instructions, as he still went curiously ranging about the shop, came as answers to his questions. She told him why the recorders used different colors of threads: the blue, as he knew, were for personal messages; the orange were for permanent storage, the yellow for use in public address systems, and the red for confidential government documents.

There were, as he also saw, various types of recorders, some of them with green plastic earphones for strictly private communications, and some so small that they would not cause a noticeable bulge in a man's hip pocket. But the sensitive mechanisms were constantly getting out of order; hence the need for many repairwomen.

"Now, if you've got the decks cleared for action," I'm ready to pitch in," proposed Chris.

Though she did not understand all his words, his meaning was clear to her; and she smilingly pointed to a work table at one end of the room.

It seemed but a few minutes later when he heard an organ-like peal at the door, and realized, with something of a shock, that Roy had returned.

"Say, old man, why couldn't you be an hour or two late?" he asked, after introducing his friend to Elva. And then to the girl, "When shall I come again? Same time tomorrow? Well, believe me, if the Plastidome doesn't fall in on us, I'll be here!"

CHAPTER XIII

No longer did Chris complain about life on Mercury. Daily he spent long hours helping Elva with her repair work, contriving methods and devices never thought of before on the planet. Or else he went with her to visit interesting spots in her Practigard, including sporting fields where the youth of the land exercised in games resembling tennis, football, and baseball; and the huge theatre, with its roof open to the Plastidome, where plays were performed by government actors for all citizens without charge.

"But should I let her be seen with me?" he began to wonder, observing how people shrank from them wherever they went. He saw how the women would draw up their tunics, and turn their backs with little shocked cries, and how the men pushed away with brassy looks in their glittering little eyes.

"I get you in wrong everywhere," he told her one

day. "For your sake, we'd better not go out together any more."

"Oh, no, no!" she protested, and he felt a warm tug at his arm. "It is worth it, Chris! What do I care what those foolish mennen and women say?"

From the admiring warmth of her violet-blue eyes, he was sure that she meant just what she said. But this only confirmed his belief that they should not be seen together.

"What's getting into you, old fellow?" Roy asked one day, after they had been on Mercury a month. "Sometimes you've got such a faraway, dreamy look I hardly recognize you any more. Not homesick, are you?"

"What about you?" Chris countered. "Why, just a few minutes ago you were staring at the blank walls so steadily I wondered if they were an art gallery. By the way, how you getting on with *her?*"

Roy mumbled something under his breath.

He was thinking of the events of the last few weeks. He had been asked to speak at several meetings of the Octagon Branch of the Women's Concurrent Party, at which Verne had presided. And though he couldn't remember that he had said much of importance, always he had been cheered enthusiastically. Better still, he had had many conferences with Verne, in order, she said, to decide the subjects of his discussions. But all that he could recall of their talks, was the flash and sparkle of two sea-blue eyes.

Then one day Verne had met him with a happy

toss of her long flaxen curls, and announced, "I have for you good news, Roy King. All the other branches of the Women's Concurrent Party, they want to hear you too. Altogether, there are twenty-two of them."

"Twenty-two? How can I speak to twenty-two branches?"

"Oh, but you understand not! You make not twenty-two speeches. You make only one."

"On the planety Earth," she rushed on, while he stared at her uncomprehendingly, "maybe they have made not the Man-Multiplier. It is a wonderful inventioning, which is used much in politicking. Wait! You will see!"

The Man-Multipliers, as Roy soon learned, were really composed of two inventions. The first was but a "string recordifier," which took down words and duplicated them on dozens of recording threads. But the more important part of the invention was quite new to him.

One day, at Verne's invitation, he visited a darkened studio, where half a dozen men stood with instruments on tripods, like cameras with curved red lenses, though their tiny electronic tubes made them look more like radio sets. One of the men took much time in instructing Roy where and in what attitude to stand, while the red lenses were pointed at him from in front and behind and on both sides. Then, at a signal, the room blazed with almost unendurable brillance.

"Good! Now, Mr. Roy King, you have been multiplied," said the director of the cameras, after the light had flashed out. But to Roy this meant nothing until, a day or two later, he was shown a dummy resembling him so closely that he almost thought he was gazing at his living double.

"You see!" Verne pointed out, triumphantly. "The Man-Multiplier, it takes your picture on all sides, in three dimensions, exactly life-size and life-color. From this our artists, using a special pliable plastic, they build your image to look exactly like you. We can make as many copies of you as we wish. This time there will be twenty-two."

"Lord in heaven!" cried Roy, swaying with a momentary dizziness. "What will you do with twenty-two?"

"One for each of our Branches, when you your speech make from the string recordifier. It will be just the same as having you there yourself. Now, notice!"

She pulled a switch, which was wired to the dummy. And the figure opened its mouth, rolled its eyes, moved its arms, and stamped back and forth like a speaker on a platform.

"Didn't I tell you? I can make you do just what I want!" she exclaimed. "When your speech is made by the recordifier, somebody in a secret room, he will be pulling the wires. And nobody, nobody else will know that Roy King, he is not there himself. So you can twenty-two speeches make all at one time! This will multiply more than your speeches. It will multiply your popularity."

Such, in fact, proved to be the case. Roy's appearances at the twenty-two Branches were made before such huge crowds that there was not room for everyone who sought admittance, and each of the addresses had to be repeated several times. It was even said that many nonmembers of the Concurrent Party had thrust themselves into the audience.

All the while, the Air Voice was repeating old rumors.

"Many mennen and women," it announced one morning, while Roy and Chris listened, fascinated, "they are saying that our Earth visitor Mr. Roy King, he is the Light Bearer of the legend, the giant with the blue eyes and hair of the color of flax, who would come down here from the planety Earth, and many blessings upon us shower. Everywhere the people, they are hailing him as the great protectioner we have for five hundred years been waiting to see."

"Lordy, O Lordy!" Chris burst out. "What shall I do? Get down on my knees before Your Majesty?"

"I'm not fool enough to be taken in by those gabbling geese," disclaimed Roy as he turned to the *"Morning Break"* and stuffed down a pale silvery concoction so rapidly that he seemed in danger of choking.

"Wiser men than either of us have been taken in by gabbling geese. You know, really, I'm getting alarmed about you, old fellow. After all, you've got nothing but a human head—and if these Mercurites keep swelling it up for you, it'll burst. Sorry to say it, but I ought to get you off this planet at record speed."

Roy was silent for a moment. "Quite seriously, old man," he finally admitted, "though I hate to think of it, I suppose we should be figuring on our return flight. We do owe it to the Space Authority. But we might arrange to come back for a longer stay."

Chris sighed. "Lord knows, I don't want to leave just now. As you say, we might plan to come back. At any rate, we'd never forgive ourselves if we forgot our duty and lingered on. What we ought to do is take some good photographs, collect a few souvenirs, then bow our polite good-byes."

"Easier said than done!" argued Roy, as he scraped the remains of their breakfast into a chute marked *"Trash Disposaling."* "It would be the devil's own job to get back to the spaceship, out there in the airless ice fields, if they held back their permission."

"Well, at least, we can try for the permission," proposed Chris, a little doubtfully. "Let's see, how would we go about it? You might speak a message into one of those blue threads and send it to the Bureaudent."

"Guess I might," conceded Roy, with no show of alacrity.

He turned to a little green button just beneath

the door, under which were the words *"Postal Serv-icing."* "Suppose I ought to press this?"

Sometime later, after a little old native had ar-rived with a blue recording thread, Roy composed the message, with Chris' assistance:

"To His Esteemed Honor, the Bureaudent, greet-ings! This is Roy Bentley. My friend and I have been a month already in your wonderful world. We are grateful for your kind treatment and wish we could remain. But our people at home have expected us to be on the way back long before this. So with great regret we ask you kindly to provide means for our return to the spaceship *Rocket Age.*"

"Well, that ought to do it," said Chris, biting his lower lip grimly.

Impatiently they awaited the answer, which ar-rived much later in the day, on an unusually long piece of confidential government red thread. Roy's hands trembled as he adjusted the recorder.

"To my dear friend Roy King, greetings!" the Bureaudent began—though the voice, obviously, was not his. "Your message with great pain has filled me. Not for five hundred years have we a visit had from the planety Earth, and you must make not your stay so short. The people, they would allow it not. If I let you go, they would cry out even against me, their Bureaudent, and blame me for letting them lose the Light Bearer, the protectioner of the old legend. So I cannot permission you to leave.

"Nevertheless, I wish to deny not the people of

the planety Earth some news of their sister planety Mercury. So, by the grace of my high office, I permission this. Your friend the Koskuff, he may leave whenever he wishes. The time, it cannot be too soon. Let me know when he will go, and it will be my pleasure to provide a Government Practigard at once to take him back to the spaceship."

There was silence for a moment.

"By glory," Chris at last found voice, "what a nice diplomatic way to kick a fellow out!"

"Think I'd let you go all by yourself?" demanded Roy, as his tall, lean form shuffled uneasily about the room.

"Think I'd let you stay here all by yourself?" flung back Chris. "No, old man, we've been through a lot together, and for better or worse, together we stick!"

"You bet we do!" affirmed Roy, throwing one arm companionably about Chris's shoulders. "Well, at least we've done our best. Now we'll have to figure out something else. Meanwhile, it looks like we're stuck on Mercury."

"Sure does look like we're trapped!"

But neither man expressed any further complaints.

CHAPTER XIV

The spacemen jerked themselves to attention where they sat side by side in their room, their legs stretched out before them as their listened to the Air Voice.

". . . Now for the sensation of the day," the Voice was saying. "This, of course, continues to be Roy King's book, 'History of the Planety Earth Since the Hydrogen Death.' The Government printographers, they are unable to roll out copies enough. A new edition of ten thousand, it is on the way. Most people, they agree with the review of Marigold Harreys in the *Purple Sheet,* that it is a most great work of history, which could only by a man of genius be written. Mr. King, he was just today voted the Green Plastic of Literary Merit by the Daughters of the Plastidome. . . ."

"Whew!" Roy could not help breaking out.

"Green Plastic of Literary Merit! That's a new one on me!"

"Who'd of thought it," applauded Chris, rising and patting his friend jocularly on the shoulder. "Here I've been pals with a great writer, and never even suspected it!"

"There are rumorings," the Voice went on, "that still more honors, they are being planned for Mr. King, who is being hailed more and more as the Light Bearer. But more about that later. First our Circulator, he has something of interest for all mennen and women. Have you equipped your Practigard with a Doodle Bivalve Triple-Speed Hopper? Doodle gives the mostest for the leastest . . ."

"Well, that's that!" decided Chris, as he snapped off the Air Voice. "If any more honors are heaped on you, old chap, I won't be able to touch you with a ten-foot pole."

He sauntered over to a table and idly picked up a shining metallic object about as long as his forearm and a little wider than his palm. For the hundredth time, his eyes fell upon the words that stood out in luminous letters, "History of the Planety Earth . . ."

"They sure do a neat book job," he mused. "Believe me, I'll take this copy back home for a souvenir."

Turning the silvery first sheet for the twentieth time, he stared at an idealized picture of Roy, in which he looked, as Chris wryly remarked, "like a cross between Sir Galahad and the angel Gabriel."

Chris turned a little switch, and the picture moved, bowing and gesticulating as in actual life. He turned another switch, and Roy's voice came forth: "Mennen and women, great pleasure I take in introducizing you to the history of the planety Earth—"

"The damned fake!" Roy broke in. "It isn't even my voice. It's done by professional actors."

"Just the same, sounds mighty like you, old fellow. I must say these Mercurites are clever, fitting up every book with a small movie reproducer and a tiny phonograph."

"Too damned clever. I'm told lots of folks never read the books—just buy them for the sound and pictures." Roy yawned, glanced at his watch, then shot up with a start. "Heavens! It's about time! I'm to be the guest, you know, at another meeting of the Women's Concurrents."

"Wonder what new honors they'll shovel out," Chris meditated, as Roy hastily groomed himself. "Whatever happens, old pal, save me a place near enough to lick your boots."

About a week later, Chris returned to their room to find Roy excitedly pacing back and forth.

"Say, old man, what's the meaning of this?" Roy greeted him, a little shocked. "Didn't take a chance, and come back all by yourself, did you? Why, if you were caught breaking the Bureaudent's rules—"

"Oh, the old duck can go take a swim in the lake!" growled Chris, with a defiant forward thrust of his well-formed lower jaw. "I've decided it's time for me to stop going around with a nursemaid. Of course, I'm taking chances. But I've noticed everybody makes out not to see me, and keeps at a distance, so I think I'll get away with it."

"Hope so. I'd hate to have to visit you in the—the Lockuppery. You know, I was just about to go to Elva's for you. There's something I want to talk over with you."

"Good. Not planning any more books?"

"Heaven forbid! But this new matter, well—" He hesitated, and looked embarrassed. "This does spring out of that damned book. You know how crazy everybody's gone—all the messages and invitations I've gotten. Worst of it is, lots of these idiots do believe I'm a sort of fabulous monster called the Light Bearer—"

"Yes, yes, I know," Chris broke in, hastily. "But if you don't get to the point, old sport, I'll die from an attack of acute impatience."

Roy remained stockstill for a moment, pulling absently at his flaxen locks, which, for the sake of effect, he had allowed to remain so long that they half buried his ears.

"What would you say," he blurted out, "if I was to run for Head Planicrat?"

"Run for—Head Planicrat!" Chris broke into a howl. "I'd say you're even crazier than I thought!"

"Most likely," Roy agreed. "Just the same, I mean it."

Chris's electric-blue eyes blazed. "Trying to kid me, old fellow? Or somebody kidding you?"

"Nobody's kidding anybody. Sit down, and I'll tell you all about it. I've got to decide right off whether or not to accept. That's why I want a serious talk."

"I'll be as serious as a gravedigger," conceded Chris, seating himself opposite his partner. But his eyes twinkled.

"I guess you know there'll be a Planicrat election in a month or two. The old Planicrat, being overage, can't run again," explained Roy, nervously drawing up his long legs. "The Men's Concurrent Party needs a candidate—and I've been asked to head the ticket."

Chris struggled with the threatened laughter. "Well, believe me, you're making progress, old fellow. What did you do? Hypnotize the natives?"

"If you'll listen, and skip the wisecracks, maybe you'll learn something," muttered Roy. And then, leaning far back, with his hands clasped together over his flaxen hair, "I know this sounds pretty far-fetched, but a delegation from the Men's Concurrent Party, under that guy Henry Jones—"

"You mean, our old friend, Hennery Jon-ess?"

"That's him. He's the Secretary of the Men's Concurrent Party, and he came to see me, saying that what they needed was a winning candidate, and I was sure-fire, being so confounded popular, now that everybody's reading my book—"

"What in tarnation do you know about the Men's Concurrent Party? What's their principles? Their platform?"

Roy shrugged. "Haven't the faintest idea, old fellow. I might make inquiries, of course, if you're dying to know."

"Well, from what Elva was saying," ruminated Chris, throwing back his mop of red hair with a decisive toss, "there's only one difference between Concurrent and Dissident. The Concurrent Party is the one now in office. The Dissident is the one that hopes to be in office."

"That's difference enough for me," decided Roy. "I'm all for the Concurrents anyway, since Verne is one of them. I couldn't very well refuse to run, could I, seeing that she sort of asked me to?"

Chris let out a snort. "No, not if the sweet lady asked you. But why, in Pete's name, are you consulting me?" Absently he snatched a sheet of silvery metallic native paper from the table; with an angry wrench, he tore it into two; then rumbled on. "Still, some things about this smell pretty fishy, old chap. First of all, who'd be running against you?"

"A guy named Frederick—rather, Fred-dericke Wil-lemson. They say he doesn't amount to much. The Dissidents had to put him in because he contributed so many Mercures to their campaign."

"All right, then. Just for the sake of argument, suppose you're crazy enough to run, and are elected? What happens then? How're we ever going to get loose from this planet if you're tied down here as Planicrat?"

"I've thought of that. But the way I look at things is this. As it is now, I haven't a ghostly chance to be released. But as an official, I could pull ropes."

"And maybe hang yourself on them. Of course, you might appoint yourself Mercurite ambassador to the Earth!" gibed Chris. And then, crumbling the remains of the silvery paper into a wad and tossing it neatly into a chute halfway across the room, he rushed on, "Next point I'd like to know is this. You're only a foreigner on Mercury, you know. Not even a naturalized citizen. So how in heck are you eligible for one of the highest offices?"

"I've thought of that too, old man," stated Roy as he began ambling about the room, his hands clasped together behind him. "I asked Henry Jones—"

"Jon-ess," corrected Chris, with an impish grimace.

"Anyway, I asked him. He said the lawyers had taken that up. They went through all their books and couldn't find any law against men from another planet holding office. Of course, the Dissidents threaten to bring this up in court; but Jones said not to worry, my term of office would probably be up long before the judges came to a decision."

"But what the devil do you know, old fellow, about the office of Head Planicrat? Any more than I know, let's say, about translating Confucius?"

"Never said I knew anything about it," Roy defended, his large blue eyes showing a troubled glint. "But Jones claims that's no disadvantage. He says I'm not expected to know a damned thing. All I'd have to do is preside at meetings, sign papers, and appoint under-Planicrats to tackle the real work."

"Well then, old man, the opening's cut out just for you!" laughed Chris.

But at this Roy bristled. "What the deuce is getting into you today, with all your jabs and objections? Haven't thought up any more questions, have you?"

Chris stared at his partner anxiously. "Well, I hate to seem fussy, but I do have some more. Just between you and me, old pal, I'm wondering if you're not forgetting some of the damn-fool customs of this planet. Don't you know that the winner for Head Planicrat has to marry the winner for Women's Planicrat?"

"Yes, but maybe you don't realize who's running for Women's Planicrat? They tell me Verne has a clear road ahead."

"Oh, now I begin to see light!" Chris bent double with laughter. "Well, I congratulate you! Verne is a lovely girl. I commend your choice. I hate, however, to have to throw cold water on your bright plans, but maybe it just hasn't occurred to you that your dear friend won't be unopposed."

Roy glowered.

"Maybe you'll also want my congratulations, old

fellow, if Marigold comes out first. Of course, tastes differ—"

He left the sentence eloquently unfinished.

"But *how* can she come out first?" Roy demanded, savagely. "Why, you can see for yourself, she doesn't hold a candle to a beautiful, smart girl like Verne! Everybody says she hasn't the tail end of a chance. All the less so since Verne is the Bureaudent's granddaughter."

"Well, let's hope you're right," conceded Chris. "If your mind's made up, I guess it's made up. Of course, you can count on me to root for you, old man. I'll even do some campaigning—"

"Not if you're my friend!" Roy refused, making a wry face. "I sure appreciate your intentions, but that would be the one thing that would positively beat me."

Chris groaned. "Oh, I'd forgotten; I'm a Koskuff. But don't let that stand in the way. For your sake, I might make speeches praising the other side."

Roy glanced at his wrist watch, then hastened on: "In just about half an hour, I'll have to give Jones my decision. Let's see, he said take Tubelator Eleven. They want to start their publicity campaign right away. . . ."

Chris, having turned to glance out of the window toward the street where Practigards were hopping, bit his lip, and contracted his bushy brow with a troubled expression.

CHAPTER XV

Swinging a tool that was half screwdriver and half pliers, Chris bent over a little machine strung with a grass-green thread. "Well, I have this licked," he said, glancing up with an understanding smile into Elva's sparkling violet-blue eyes.

She glanced across at him happily, and brushed aside the long dark hair that reached almost to her shoulders.

"Chris, this is enough for today," she decided. "You are such a help, I still think I am the most luckiest girl on Mercury."

"And I'm the luckiest man. You don't know what you've meant to me, Elva," he answered, coming close to her, with a yearning smile.

"It's almost time to go to the Ellipse," she broke in. "In my Practigard, I will take you there."

The Ellipse, he knew, was a great auditorium reserved for public discussions. This afternoon it was to be the scene of the most important meeting in the election campaign, when the candidates for Head Planicrat and Women's Planicrat were all to be heard. In recognition of the occasion, a half holiday had been declared, and people who could not crowd into the Ellipse were to listen over the Air Voice.

"You know, Elva," Chris pleaded, "I'd just as soon stay here, pottering around with these machines."

"Oh, but Chris, you *must* go!" Elva insisted, in her soft, rich voice. "It is something worth knowing about. Besides, you must see your friend Roy King."

"I can see Roy often enough without watching him make a public monkey of himself," grumbled Chris. "Not that I've seen him very much of late. Now that the campaign's on, he's hardly in our room at all. And even when he is there, he's busy listening to those darned messages on the string recorder—usually enough of them to tie a man hand and foot."

"You should be proud of Roy," remonstrated Elva. "Everybody says he is a great campaignifier. But come! If we are late, maybe we will get not into the Ellipse."

Half an hour later, having left her Practigard on the lowest floor of a ten-story building crowded with parked machines, Elva led the way to an immense egg-shaped edifice rising a hundred feet toward the Plastidome, and glowing throughout with a faint milkish illumination. Chris noticed that there were dozens of doors, and rows of minute round windows like the portholes of a ship.

Toward this building people were swarming from multitudes of Practigards; Elva and Chris found every seat already taken, and many people were standing in the aisles. The interior, Chris saw, somewhat resembled that of an old Greek amphitheatre, with vast semicircular rows of seats, and an enormous platform or stage on which dozens of chairs had been placed. But what was that faint, peculiar, sweetish-sharp odor, reminding the Earthman a little of peppermint?

"Most lucky are we, Chris!" exclaimed Elva, with an enthusiastic tug at his arm. "See! We are in!"

"Yes, my girl, but it won't be any fun for you, having to stand all the time."

But all at once he saw that they would not have to stand. The people in the nearest seats were staring at him with sidelong glances and horrified gasps and mutterings. Then, one by one, they edged away. Soon a circle ten feet wide had been cleared between him and the nearest Mercurite.

"Well, if they don't want the seats, that's their loss," he decided, and led Elva to two comfortable-looking chairs right next to a great white roof-supporting column on the highest row of seats. "There sure are some advantages in being a Koskuff."

But so much noise was dinning all about them that she could not hear him. Children were whooping up and down the aisle, rattling instruments that looked like castanets, or blowing whistles and horns. Loud-speakers were blaring announcements. And from time to time, at one end of the hall, a machine resembling a pile driver crashed down upon a metallic base. "That is to wake the right spirit in the people," Elva explained, during a brief pause in the clamor.

All along the walls, placards were strung. "Vote for the Mennen's Concurrent Party!" "Vote for the Mennen's Dissident Party!" "Vote for Verne Wyle, and Wisdom in Government!" "Vote for Marigold Har-reys, and a Good Business Bureaustration!" Pictures of the leading candidates, on metal plaques, were dispersed among the other placards; but Chris could not recognize either Roy or Verne in the portraits.

"Ah, now it begins!" cried Elva, making her meaning plain by excited gestures. The commotion had become so loud that Chris's ears were aching. "O-way! O-way! Way-o! Wheek! Wheek! Wheek! O-way! Way-o! Wheek! Wheek! Wheek!" On both sides of the stage, doors had opened. From the right, the candidates and chief officials of the Mennen's and Women's Concurrent Parties trooped in, and took seats; from the left, the officials and candidates of the Dissident Parties.

"Good Lord! Look at Roy!" Chris muttered to himself.

All the candidates were dressed in broad, colored,

loose-flowing robes, which covered them from the shoulders to the knees. And Roy's robe, of scarlet and black, was particularly striking, the more so because of his tall, dominating figure.

"O-way! O-way! Way-o! Wheek! Wheek! Wheek!" the applause roared on. Then all at once, as suddenly as if a switch had been turned off, it ceased and made way for an announcement from the loud-speakers.

"Now we will hear the mottos of the parties! First, the Mennen's Concurrent!"

Like a thunder burst, these words blared forth:

"Hearty! Hearty! Hearty! Hearty!
Vote the Mennen's Concurrent Party!"

A dozen times the words were repeated, while hundreds of voices chanted the syllables in unison and each pause was punctuated by a tremendous thumping of the machine like a pile driver.

"Lord in heaven! What's the sense of it?" Chris demanded of Elva. But she was unable to explain until later that the mottos were spoken not for their sense, but for their hypnotic effects, it having been found by experiment that eight-four and seventy-seven one hundredths per cent of the people were moved by anything blared at them often enough.

Next came the Women's Concurrents, whose motto was

"We are the daughters, sisters, mothers,
    We are the daughters, sisters, mothers,
    We are the daughters, sisters, mothers . . ."

That was all there was to it; but when repeated fifteen or twenty times, and chanted by a great audience of women, it seemed an utterance of profound wisdom.

The mottos of the Dissident Parties were of exactly the same kind, and while they were being recited, Chris's attention began to wander. He had noticed a series of small perforations, no larger than the openings in the nozzle of a hose, which stretched in long even rows along the white column above him. Beneath the perforations, a foot or two overhead, there was a little knob with a numbered dial beside it. He wondered what these were, but the noise prevented him from asking.

Then once more the loud-speakers spoke, with a stertorous voice that drowned all other sounds: "Now, before the ceremonialings begin, those that wish, they may step up and handshake the candidates!"

Instantly there was a rush toward the stage, in which it seemed that thousands participated. Amid the crush, several women were trampled and had to be rescued by ushers who stood by with first-aid equipment. "O-way! O-way! Way-o! Wheek! Wheek! Wheek!" the applause rang forth.

"Don't you want to go up and shake your friend's

hand?" asked Elva, when after a time the applause had died down sufficiently for her to be heard.

"What for?" Chris gasped. "Why, I can whack him on the back any time I want to! Of course—" he paused, and hesitated—"maybe you'd like to do some handshaking—"

"Not me!" she refused, crisply. "No, not after what I have been told, I would not handshake any candidate."

He wondered what it was that put the sparkling amusement into her eyes. But just then the uproar grew so loud again that he could not ask.

Across the rear of the stage a rope had been thrown, and from each side, through a special door, the people began filing in a continuous line on moving platforms that never stopped for an instant; meanwhile, the crowds were held back by the rope, against which they pressed and surged. The candidates had ranged themselves on the opposite side of the rope, Roy and Verne to the right, and Marigold and Fred-dericke Wil-lemson to the left. And as the people drifted by, each person in turn reached out a hand, which was shaken in a quick grip. The contact in no case could have lasted more than a second. But the men and women trooping back from the stage walked gingerly, with elation in their eyes.

It was nearly an hour before the handshaking was all over, and meanwhile Chris's head had begun to ache. That peculiar peppermint smell in the air was more noticeable than ever. But he peered all about him, and could see no one who seemed to be eating candy or chewing gum.

Then a long new round of applause broke out as the Budeaudent came on to the platform and stood bowing. Chris recognized him at once: the five-foot form, the colorless eyes behind their bags of fat, and the bland round face on which a perpetual grin seemed pasted. His skin, beneath the reddish bald pate, had its usual ruddy tinge. But there was one peculiar thing: he looked much younger than before.

"The old boy sure looks well," Chris remarked to Elva, after the applause had died down sufficiently for conversation.

She smiled in delicious, unconcealed amusement. "But it is not he at all. It's only one of his multiples," she revealed. "The Bureaudent, he can come not to every meeting. He has been multiplied a hundred times, so he may be seen wherever he is needed. This, it saves so much of his time and energy."

She went on to explain that the dummy was pulled by wires attached to a switchboard behind the stage, which controlled every movement and gesture. His speech, needless to say, came from a "string recordifier," which was connected with loud-speakers throughout the hall, and with the Air Voice. "I learned this all when I worked with the Multipliers," Elva explained. "But most of the people, they know it not."

At the conclusion of his speech, the Bureaudent's

multiple introduced Roy, whom he hailed as "the Light Bearer, the great man from the planety Earth." Roy then stepped forth, after another din of applause. But Chris, as he saw his friend gesticulating, knew that he also spoke from a recordifier."

Then the supposed Bureaudent got up again, and introduced his granddaughter, Verne. And when she in turn arose, bowing low and beaming out of her sea-blue eyes, Chris could not help reflecting, "By gum! I can't blame Roy! But no," he ruminated, as his gaze wandered to the filed, blade-like face of Marigold, who sat stiffly at the head of the Dissidents. "If I were in his place, I wouldn't risk it, not if there was a chance in a million of getting that other one instead."

Verne's speech was short and apt, and was applauded tumultuously. And now the Bureaudent— or, rather, his multiple—arose to introduce Marigold, whom he praised as "one of the most renownified circulators on the planety Mercury, a forward-looking woman, who, though I may not with her agree politically, I much admire personally. . . ." There was more in the same vein, while Marigold could be seen puffing herself up like a hen, smoothing down her hair, and fidgeting in her seat as she made ready for her speech. Her normally waxen face had taken on a ruddy glow.

Chris's attention meantime had wandered; he wished he had never come to this tiresome meeting. His eyes traveled to the white column just above him, and the little red knob with the numbered dial; and he wondered what this might be. Then, absently, more because he was bored than for any other reason, he began fingering the dial, and found that a small button beneath it turned easily at his touch, accompanied by movements of the needle in the dial. He twisted the button from left to right, until it would turn no further, and was about to swing it back when he again noticed that queer peppermint odor in the air, sharper and more pungent than before.

Then a peculiar thing happened. All about him the people had begun to sneeze suddenly and violently. At his side, Elva likewise sneezed. He turned toward her, and he himself sneezed, with such force that his whole body jerked forward. At the same time his right hand, which had been gripping the button beneath the dial, gave an involuntary lunge, pulling the button away with him and tearing it out of its fastenings. And as he glanced back at the dial, he saw that the needle was oscillating furiously, as if it had gone crazy.

Just then he sneezed again—sneezed several times in uncontrollable succession. That peppermint odor was now so strong that it seemed to be tearing at his nostrils, his eyes, his throat; seemed to burn and scourge his lungs. "By the Plastidome, Chris, what have you done?" he heard Elva's dismayed cry. Then other cries came from all about him—screams of pain and terror. There was a sudden thudding of feet, a wild rush as men and women made for the exits. With incredible rapidity, the rush spread; in a moment, all that could be seen was a pandemonium of savage, pushing forms, screaming, screeching, shouting, howling, and yelling like penned beasts.

Then, even above the clamoring of the mob, there came the shriek of a siren—three piercing emergency blasts. And following these dread sounds, while the uproar of the multitude momentarily died to a low wailing, there came the thunderous voice of the loud-speakers, "Be calm, mennen and women! Walk to the nearest entrance! The danger, we will overcome it! Be calm! Be calm!"

With a loud flapping, the portholes all along the building suddenly opened. And the doors swung wide; and the mobs, gasping and coughing, moved out with a surge and thrust. Chris, too, was gasping and coughing; that peppermint seemed to be asphyxiating him; his eyes smarted, and his head was a fury of pain. But somehow he managed to seize Elva's hand, and to hold it while the two of them, sputtering and struggling for breath, forced their way through the terrible press of bodies out into the reviving air of the street.

CHAPTER XVI

It was long before Elva, amid the confusion, could find her Practigard, and hop away with Chris at her side. Both of them, their clothes ruffled by the crowd, felt as if someone had slugged them in the head. But by the time they had returned to her workshop, the fumes were clearing away, though they were still red-faced and flustered.

"I was so afraid for you, Chris," Elva finally said, after she had prepared him a soothing drink of a beverage called "Marg," which tasted a little like tea. "If that mob knew what you did, they would tear you to bits!"

"But just what did I do?" he asked as he sat opposite her sipping the drink. "I still don't understand. All I remember is turning that dial. I couldn't help sneezing. It wasn't my fault, was it, if the contraption broke?"

"The—what do you call it, the contraption?—

maybe you know not what it was," she said, smiling faintly, and throwing back her long straight-combed dark hair with a hasty toss. "The contraption—it regulated the Oozodine."

"What in heck is Oozodine?"

"So you have it not on the planety Earth? But we on Mercury, we use it at many public meetings. It is a drug which into the air we spray in small quantities. Did you notice not the peculiar sharp, sweetish smell?"

"Sure did. But what's the idea, Elva, spraying a drug into the air?"

"It is what we call a placidifier. It placidifies people's minds so they will be in a more ready mood for what they hear. Psychologists, they have proved it makes people fifty-nine per cent more willing to believe."

"Good Lord, what a planet!" Chris mumbled. "So a man can't even attend a political meeting without being drugged."

"But a little of the drug, it does not any harm. The dial, it was meant to control the amount, so that not too much would get into the air. But you broke the regulator; after that, there was no way to stop the flow of Oozodine. Maybe a hundred times too much got into the atmosphere. And so much Oozodine, it is a poison."

"Sure don't have to tell me," acknowledged Chris, whose nose and eyes still smarted.

"Now the great Planicrat meeting, it is ended," reflected Elva, with a sigh. "The Oozodine, it clings a long time. Nobody will be able to use the Ellipse for days—nobody! The Dissidents, how they must grumble they had not their chance to speak!"

"Yes, I can imagine the nice gentle things dear little Marigold must be saying."

"Let's hear if the Air Voice says anything," Elva went on, crossing the room, and turning a switch. "I am afraid, Chris, if anybody noticed who did it—"

"Oh, don't you worry, Elva! First everybody was busy listening to the speech, and after that they were all busier yet sneezing and coughing. What I'd like to know is how poor Roy came out."

The Air Voice now made itself heard, beginning in the middle of a broadcast:

". . . the most terrible panic since the false alarm about the break in the Plastidome. Our Circulators, they have not yet been able to learn how many were hurt.

"Meanwhile there is much disputationing about the cause. Dr. Har-rolde Smit-the, the well-known scientitioner, he says a hidden defect may have been in the Oozodine valves. Dr. Wil-lem Henneryson, Manager of the Ellipse, he says he has for a long time been suspicioning some employees, and will charges of incompetence file. Eye-leen Ell-ey-yott, Chairodent of the Daughters of the Plastidome, she claims it was sabotage by subversives among the mennen. Marigold Har-reys, of the Women's Dissidents, she says it was all a plot by the Concurrents."

"Well, at least, Chris," Elva sighed in relief, "nobody yet has mentioned you."

". . . Miss Har-reys," the Voice rumbled on, "she has great positivity shown. She says it could be not by chance that the trouble, it started just before her turn to speak. She charges that the Women's Concurrent Party, it deliberately poisoned the air. Asked by a Circulator of this station just who she suspicioned, she said she was a woman of good will and hated to accusify anybody, but a good citizen has to speak her mind for the sake of the country. She had reason to believe, she said, that the plot, it has headed by someone she would mention not by name, except that she was a close relation of the Bureaudent. This charge, it is foreseen, will have radical effects upon the campaign. . . ."

"The damned old witch!" Chris swore, stamping about the room and missing the next words of the Air Voice. "Accusing a nice, decent girl like Verne of a ratlike thing like that! What I'm afraid is that this is going to lose her the election."

"Oh, no, it is not!" denied Elva as she turned off the Air Voice, which had gone on to another subject. "Do not forget, Chris, the Bureaudent's granddaughter is very popular."

"Well, sure would be tough on Roy if she lost!" Chris rambled on, as he roved about the room, almost upsetting several "recordifiers" in his excitement. "So it looks like there's only one thing to do, unless I'm twin brother to a skunk."

"What can you do, Chris?"

"I'll have to let 'em know who did it," he resolved as he stood against a stone workbench, with chin propped thoughtfully on palm. "I'll take the consequences!"

"Oh, but Chris, what are you talking of?" Elva demanded, coming to him pleadingly. "Your wits—have they flown out of the window? Do you not see, nobody would believe you? But even if they did believe, they would say that, being a Koskuff, you deserved not to live. Then some good patriots, they would stone you to death. Or the Bureaudent, he would send the executionifier with his hypodermic, which, as they say, would 'put you to sleep.' Please, Chris, please, do not anything so foolish!"

"Now, Elva, quiet down there, just for a minute," he counseled, taking her hands and drawing her toward him. "I can't believe they'd execute a fellow simply because he made a little mistake with a dial on a wall. Tell you what! I'll speak to Roy. He'll know what to do."

"If I were you, Chris, I would speak not to Roy," she appealed. "What good can it bring you?"

But he insisted, and his intention to tell everything was uppermost in his mind when he returned to their room.

"Well, how's the future Head Planicrat?" he greeted Roy, trying to seem jovial and offhand, all the more so since Roy had slumped in without his usual buoyant good cheer.

"Pretty rotten, old fellow!" groaned Roy, as he sank into a chair. "My head—darn the useless chunk of lead!—it's aching. You don't know what I've been through. Did anybody tell you about the hullabaloo down at the Ellipse—"

"Nobody had to tell me. I was deep in it, along with Elva. Say, that sure was a phony speech you made. Why, your gesticulations didn't even match your words."

"Couldn't help it," sighed Roy, his head drooping, while he ran a weary hand across his brow. "You know how they can those speeches for you way in advance. Why, those damned words on the recorder weren't mine at all; they were written and spoken by the Spectral Speakers. All I had to do was stand there like a monkey, making gestures as though I were really speaking."

Chris threw his head back and laughed.

"Anyhow, there's one thing I did admire, old fellow, and that was the way you shook hands. How'd you keep it up for nearly an hour? I'll give you credit for endurance."

Roy made a wry face. "Afraid I can't take any credit there, either. Maybe I'm giving a state secret away, but I'll let you in on something. I didn't shake one darned hand."

"No? Then I was suffering from hallucinations?"

"I didn't say that," drawled Roy. "You see, old boy, it's like this. Sometime ago they found that candidates wore themselves out shaking hands. One

nominee suffered a sprained wrist. Another had a
dislocated shoulder. Still another died from a heart
attack. So they set their inventors to work. Maybe
you noticed those broad mantles we wore? Well, we
each had an artificial arm hidden under the mantle.
The hand was made of synthetic rubber, with a heat-
ing system and a thermostat keeping it at skin tem-
perature; and it looked darned natural. Even the
finger joints, which had little steel rods inside,
worked just like normal. When I wanted to shake a
hand, all I had to do was press a concealed button
connecting with a battery, and the hand would
stretch out, and shake. When I pressed the button
again, the hand would shoot back under the mantle.
Of course, nobody ever guessed they were really
shaking a machine's hand."

"What a fake!" Chris muttered.

"I wouldn't call it that. Just a labor-saving device.
After all, what did it matter whose hand those folks
shook so long as they *thought* it was mine?"

For a moment, Chris was silent. "Listen here, old
fellow," he changed the subject, "there's a question
I want to ask you. Think this breakup of the meeting is going to hurt your chances?"

"Why should it?"

"Well, that old crow Marigold, over the Air
Voice—"

"Aw, who in thunder cares for that croaking bird?
Yes, I know, she's been blaming poor Verne. But
who'll believe her? Why, in the straw votes—

dummy votes, they call them here—Verne's ahead
four to one."

"Hope she keeps her lead. Just the same, old
fellow, I've got a confession to make, even if you'll
take me for the world's Number One fool."

Roy's face twisted into an amused grimace. "What
you been up to now? Can I still not trust you out of
sight?"

"Afraid not. Just listen to this—then you can
curse me all you want to."

And so he took a seat opposite Roy, and told his
story.

But until the recital was over, the grin of amusement did not leave Roy's face. Then, slapping one
knee with a resounding whack, he roared, "Boy, you
sure messed things up fine! How'd you manage it
so neatly? Believe me, that'll be something to tell
about back on earth!"

"Well, go ahead, bawl me out, why don't you?"
Chris challenged. "Say I'm the lousiest, looniest partner a spaceman ever had! Say I've fouled the gears
for you and Verne in this election—"

"Aw, don't you worry about the election," advised
Roy, clapping his friend heartily about the shoulders. "As I've been trying to pound into your thick
skull, this won't matter one straw. Why, Verne and
I have that other gang licked so bad they haven't a
look-in—"

"Wish I could be sure of that. But the Air Voice,
old fellow—I heard it over at Elva's, and it said this

would make a radical difference in the campaign."

"Radical bologna! Verne told me all about the Air Voice. The announcer is paid to keep saying something, and if he doesn't know what to dish out, he simply makes up some guff."

"But what if this isn't guff? You may think I'm crazy," concluded Chris, "but I won't feel I've done the decent thing till I've made a clean breast of it. Got a piece of that recording thread, old chap?"

"What for?" asked Roy, as he opened a wall partition and drew out a blue thread.

Chris did not answer, but strung the thread on the "recordifier" and began to speak: "To His Excellency, the Bureaudent . . ."

CHAPTER XVII

"Marigold Har-reys accusifies! Marigold Har-reys accusifies! Read all about the electioning scandal! Marigold makes great revelationing! Accusifies the Concurrents! Read the *Purple Sheet*. All about the scandal!"

These words stared on immense placards above a pile of purple-bordered silvery papers in an open space or Circle at the intersection of two streets. Just at this point Elva had halted her Practigard, and, with Chris beside her, sat staring at the gaudy red, white, and yellow striped newsstand.

"I must a paper buy," she said, with an air of nervous excitement. And she hopped out of the Practigard and quickly returned with her purchase, at which she glanced with deepening concern. "Back to my shop we must hurry!"

They started off again, alternately gliding in air and jolting along the pavement. But at a cross street they were halted by a traffic jam, and during the wait Elva's eyes returned to the *Purple Sheet*.

"I usually buy not this paper," she said. "It is what we call a sick sheet, for it tells of everything unhealthy—which, they say, is why it is so popular. I am afraid of it, Chris."

"Oh, don't be disturbed by the croakings of that old raven, Marigold."

"It is not only her. Did you—tell me—did you message the Bureaudent?"

"Sure!" he answered, with a start. "Must have been a week ago. Guess the old boy's been too busy to answer. But who the deuce told you?"

The Practigard just ahead of them jerked forward, then jolted to a stop amid a fog of evil-smelling smoke. Elva automatically had moved her hands to the controls.

"Nobody has told me, Chris. But I have rumorings heard. Rumorings that you to the Bureaudent said that the trouble at the Ellipse, it was all made by you. People everywhere, they are talking about it. But they believe it not."

A puzzled look had entered Chris's electric-blue eyes.

"I don't quite get that, Elva. Here I send the Bureaudent a private message. Nobody knows about it except him and Roy, who wouldn't tell. So how does this story get out?"

The Practigard ahead of them jerked forward again, letting out a cloud of green gas.

"These waits, I hate them so much, sometimes I wish Practigards had never been invented," Elva confided. "But about your story, Chris. Maybe you know it not, but the Bureaudent, he gets so many messages he can hear them not all himself. So he has a Listening Clerk, who lets him know what he should hear."

"Good Lord! Then maybe he didn't get my letter!"

"Maybe not. But the Listening Clerk, she heard it—and that was a piece of news which maybe she could keep not to herself. After all, a Listening Clerk, she is only human."

"And if she told just one person, the whole planet knows," Chris concluded, with a groan. "Now I see what a damned fool I was!"

"You were not a fool—you knew not our customings," Elva defended. "Still, I'm afraid. Much afraid, Chris. We will see when we read the *Purple Sheet*."

Just then the Practigard ahead of them shot forward, amid a blur of green gas that half choked and blinded them. Until they were safely back at her shop, the difficulties of travel prevented further conversation. Then, for the first time, she showed Chris the three-inch headlines of the *Purple Sheet*:

MARIGOLD HAR-REYS CHARGES
ELECTIONING PLOT
ACCUSIFIES WOMEN'S CONCURRENT PARTY
Exclusive by MARIGOLD HAR-REYS
Staff Circulator, *The Purple Sheet*

"What a lot of darned scareheads!" Chris scoffed.
"From the little I know of Marigold—which is a
great deal too much—this is about what I'd expect."

"Just the same, Chris, such empty words, they
move people more than the sayings of great philoso-
phers. Shall I read you the rest?"

"Please do," he requested, seating himself opposite
her.

" 'The followers of this paper,' " Elva read, in her
clear, full voice, "they know the opinioning that
many times I have expressed, that the recent trouble
at the Ellipse, it was caused by a plot of the Women's
Concurrents. But now I have proof of an even lower,
more vile conspiring.

" 'Taking fright from the loss of thousands of
votifiers, the Concurrents, they have grown desper-
ate. So they have the filthiest story told that I have
ever heard. The readers of this paper, they know that
I would be the last to say anything in favor of the
Koskuff from the planety Earth. Just the same, I am
for fair play. My blood, it boils when I see the Wom-
en's Concurrents use him as a scapegoat, forcing him
to say he was the one who has the air at the Ellipse
poisoned with Oozodine. What would a man from
the planety Earth know about Oozodine, unless
somebody told him? And who would tell him? The
story, it is so childish I would laugh if it was not such
a villainous plot to deceivify the votifiers.

" 'But here is the most dastardly part of it all. This
fraud, as I have myself veridified, has been traced

straight to the highest officer in the country, in an effort to save his grandchild from defeat. I think that
the women of Mercury, they will like not such cheat-
ing. They will show their protest by voting for the
Women's Dissidents. The party of no frauds! The
party of truth! First on the planety, first for Hu-
manity!' "

Elva threw the paper from her with a disgusted
grunt.

But Chris had shot to his feet, and began pounding the air with both fists. "What does the old hawk
mean, that I was forced to say I poisoned the air? You
know darned well, Elva, I said it of my own free
will!"

"Of course I know it, Chris," she reassured him,
coming close and putting one hand consolingly on
his arm. "But will other people know it? Won't they
think there really was a plot? So how can we keep
them from voting for Marigold?"

Chris muttered beneath his breath. "Well, looks
like I only messed things up worse by trying to set
them right," he reflected as he moved slowly about
the room. "So now it's up to me, I guess, to untangle
the tangle."

"But, Chris, how can you?"

"There must be some way. Let's see, how long is
it till the election?"

"Electioning we call it, Chris. Eleven days."

He bit his lip. "Not one minute too long. See here,
Elva, it's just come to me only one thing is possible.

Where I went wrong before was in not getting my message through to the Bureaudent. I'll have to contact him directly and tell him I'll make a public statement testifying that no one coerced me into my confession."

"But, Chris! Don't knock your head into worse trouble! How can you directly go to the Bureaudent? And even if you do, who will believe—"

"At least, I'll try. Only a skunk would lie down now, after he'd gotten Verne—and Roy—into trouble. Roy will be able to get me an interview with the Bureaudent through Verne. And she'll be all the more willing, and so will her granddad, after the vicious things Marigold said about him."

"But even if you do see the Bureaudent, and he does let you your public confession make," appealed Elva, the anxiety deepening in her eyes, "how do you know what Marigold will do? I trust not that woman. Did I not myself have much experiencing?"

"Sure did, you poor kid! But don't you worry. I'll do my darndest to make everything come out right."

An hour later, he was back in his room, where Roy had grunted a grudging approval of his idea. "I still don't think there's anything in the election to get excited about. But if you want to see the Bureaudent, why, go ahead. Verne can arrange things slick as a whistle."

Verne, however, could not arrange things "slick as a whistle." Chris told Roy the story when, looking tired but triumphant, he returned two days later from the Rhomboid.

"Been waiting around all day, old fellow," he muttered as he threw himself into a chair and began mopping the thick red locks back from his brow. "My appointment, you know, was at the sixteenth hour. But it was darned near the twenty-first when His Fussy Honor got around to me."

"Well, you did get to see him at last?"

"Oh, about halfway. A high-hatting guy in the outer office told me that a Koskuff couldn't be allowed face-to-face with His Untouchable Eminence. It was an old tradition; Koskuffs mustn't meet in the same room with the upper caste. So they put a wall between old Stuffed Shirt and me."

"No kidding? Not a real wall?"

"Looked mighty real to me. It was of transparent plastic, with a hole about as big as an apple to speak through, and it reached across the whole cursed room. His Exalted Stiffness sat on one side, and I stood on the other. I sure hope the poor fellow wasn't contaminated."

"Anyway, you said what you wanted?"

Chris had left his chair, and stood with folded arms against the wall, just to the left of the "string recordifier."

"You bet I said what I wanted. He sat listening with that grin like a stuffed baboon, and answered that he thought Verne would win hands down, no

matter what I did—still, he'd been in politics long
enough to know there were lots of tricky turns even
in the straightest road. When I mentioned Marigold,
he cursed. He said that, even if his granddaughter
wasn't running, he wouldn't leave anything under
the Plastidome unturned to defeat that old she-devil.
Maybe my help wasn't needed in the election, but
it would tickle him to see her publicly made out a
liar. So if I wanted to make a statement, he would
get me time on the Air Voice."

"Good for you, you old spellbinder!" cried Roy,
rapping Chris on the shoulder. "When do you make
your harangue?"

CHAPTER XVIII

"Let me introducize the Koskuff from the planety Earth. By special authorizing of His High Honor the Bureaudent, he speaks now in a recordified talk over the Air Voice."

Roy, seated next to Chris while these words poured out of the unseen, gave his partner a nudge. "Here goes! I'm ready for the worst!"

Strong and firm, Chris's tones rang forth from the instrument:

"Mennen and women of the planety Mercury! I am here not to defend myself, but because of a great wrong to others. A few days ago I confessed to His Excellency the Bureaudent that it was I who poisoned the air at the Ellipse. It was all an accident. I turned the control knob, not knowing what I was doing, and broke it. I am very sorry, and want to take all the blame. It is a foul lie that I was forced to make a false confession. I was not forced to make any confession. And nothing I said was false. I do not want the innocent to be blamed. I want the whole planety to know this, so that everybody may judge the truth."

"Bravo!" cried Roy, rapping his friend on the back. "You've done swell, old boy! Beats the practice speech you made before the recording! Wonder how dear old Marigold is going to like this!"

"I could have done better if I'd had more time," explained Chris. "But that was all they would allow."

"Well, believe me, it's more than the Dissidents will appreciate. This'll lose Marigold a raft of votes," decided Roy, clapping his hands together with a gleeful roar.

For two days the planet buzzed with gossip about "the Koskuff's speech." Persons interviewed at random by Circulators of the Air Voice claimed to show popular opinion sharply divided, with four people believing that Chris had told the truth to three who held that he was lying. If this was a fair sampling, Verne's election seemed safe.

And then, like a bolt, Marigold launched her reply.

She launched it over the Air Voice and in the *Purple Sheet* and other papers, at an estimated cost of thousands of Mercures (where she got the money, no one knew, though it was assumed to have come from the coffers of the Women's Dissidents). Chris, having managed to buy a copy of the *Purple Sheet* in spite of an unprecedented demand, sat with Elva as he scanned the purple-bordered silvery pages:

MARIGOLD HAR-REYS COUNTERATTACKS
ASSAILS ENEMIES' FALSE CHARGES
STICKS TO ACCUSIFYING
OF GIGANTICAL PLOT
Special to the *Purple Sheet*
By Marigold Har-reys

"Mennen and women of Mercury, before you I put my case. In all my years of politicking, never have I such dirt seen as now. I knew that the Women's Concurrents, they would into any pit sink to steal an unfair victory. But I suspected not that they would so far fall as behind a Koskuff to hide. Everybody knows you can take not the word of a Koskuff. But the word of a Koskuff, it is the only argumentation they have.

"I thought the Women's Concurrents, they were at the bottom when they forced the Koskuff to say much silliness about the trouble at the Ellipse. But now they have dug below the bottom. Now they force him to say he was forced not to say what they force him to say.

"I still protestify it is a gigantical plot. But it is even more gigantical than I had thought. Here is the proof, which before the votifiers will be placed. It is signed by three well-known members of the Women's Dissidents. I give their own report."

"Oh, that terrible woman!" Elva exclaimed, looking up from the paper, the lovely oval of her face convulsed with anger. "I knew she had some wicked trick."

"Better read on—see what the old girl's up to," advised Chris, glaring at the paper. And Elva read, aloud:

" 'This will testify that we were in the Octagon Branch of the Women's Concurrent Party day behind yesterday at the twentieth hour. We had come not to spy, but a campaign message to deliver. We had to wait in the outer office, where no one was but us. Then from inside we heard some words. We could not help knowing the voice, which had a rude Earth accent. The heavy tones were those of the Koskuff—"

"It's a lie!" Chris broke in, springing up, and pointing irately at the paper. "Why, Elva, I've never been near the Octagon Office! Besides, as you know, at the twentieth hour day before yesterday, I was right here with you—"

"I remember," acknowledged Elva, with a sigh. "But let's go on." And she read:

" 'The heavy tones were . . . of the Koskuff. He spoke in a most low voice—' "

"How could my tones be heavy if I spoke in a most low voice?" growled Chris.

Elva smiled wryly, and read on:

" 'He spoke in a most low voice, yet we were able to catch many words: "I like not to do it, Miss Wyle."

Then a woman's voice, which sounded much like that of the Concurrent candidate, it said. "But you must. Otherwise, we can explain not to the votifiers. If you wish not to be punished, you must again say you did it. . . ."

> "Clari-belle Weak-lee
> "Margre Mal-lon-ee.
> "Margre Mal-lon-ee."

"Why, just look, damn 'em! They even have photographic facsimiles of the signatures!" exclaimed Chris, peering over Elva's shoulder. "Lord —I thought we had rotten politics on earth! But these professionals up here can give us cards and spades. How do you make it out, Elva, that these three dames actually put down their names, knowing it was all a pack of lies?"

"Well, some people," groaned Elva, "they would do anything for a few Mercures. The worse of it is, this trap it is sprung at the last minute. Only six days now to the electioning! So what chance is there to refutify this lie?"

"At least, I can prove I wasn't at that darned Octagon Office!" swore Chris, raging about the room in the mood of one who would have liked to smash the crockery. "Oh, that old turkey-hen! If she wasn't a la—a woman, I'd pummel her into a pulp! But unless we do something, I'm afraid Verne's election is as good as gone."

"I much fear so," agreed Elva. "But what can we do?"

"Hadn't we better see Roy right away? You come along, Elva. I want you to join in telling him I was right here with you at the twentieth hour day before yesterday."

"I will come," acceded Elva, rising wearily. "But I think not this will help much."

As they emerged from Elva's shop, a group of teen-aged girls surged down the corridor, waving bright-colored banners. "Vote for the Women's Dissident Party! The Party of Sisterly Love! Truth, Honor, and Honesty!" In a gay chorus, the young voices chanted:

> "Justice and sanity!
> Death to all vanity!
> Choice of the planety!"

Upon seeing Chris, the girls paused, gaping at him as if he had been an escaped alligator. Some jeered, some hissed, and all shrank away. But when they had put a safe distance between themselves and him, they trooped on their way more jauntily than ever, still waving their banners, and repeating their chant:

> "Justice and sanity!
> Death to all vanity!
> Choice of the planety!"

Roy, when Chris and Elva had hastened to him in his room, appeared as cheerful as ever.

"Seen the results of the *Carmine Sheet's* latest dummy vote?" he asked.

The others nodded in the negative.

"Well, it's just come in," Roy went on, snapping a silvery page up from the table. "First the Men's Concurrent Party. Its candidate—who's now speaking—has 13,334 votes. Fred-dericke Wil-lemson, for the Men's Dissidents, has 4,136."

"Congratulations, you old vote-getting marvel!" Chris applauded, slapping the candidate on the shoulder. "But isn't that less than you had on the previous ballot?"

"Oh, only a thousand or two," Roy shrugged off the difference. "But now to the important vote. For the candidate of the Women's Concurrents—Verne, of course—there are 9,879 votes. For the Women's Dissidents—our old friend Marigold—there are 7,652. Which I consider a pretty good safe margin."

"Yes, Mr. Roy," argued Elva, anxiously, "but that is a lead of less than four to three. And Verne, she started out with four to one."

"Well, I don't say she wasn't hurt by Marigold's latest rantings," conceded Roy. "But not enough to endanger her. Just the same, let's go and get Verne's own ideas. She should be in her office at Concurrent headquarters."

"Good!" agreed Elva. "I always wanted to meet Verne."

"But will she care to meet me, old fellow?" Chris asked his chum. "After all, you know—well, I'm a Koskuff—"

"Oh, Verne hasn't any prejudices. She's the most open-minded person you'd find."

"I wouldn't doubt it, old chap. But not all the voters might be so open-minded if she was seen with me."

"Why must she be seen with you? We'll meet in an inner office, where not an eye can look on."

Somewhat uneasily, Chris assented. But his anxiety was not relieved a little later when the three of them had left Elva's Practigard near the Concurrent headquarters. As they slipped in through a rear entrance, Chris thought that he noticed something skulking behind them; and turned just in time to see a small, plump, vaguely familiar figure. "Who in the devil's name can it be?" he wondered. "Shucks! Am I getting so scary I jump at every shadow?"

Inside the building, they sensed the excitement. As Verne was not in her office, they had to wait; and meanwhile they heard agitated scurryings, whisperings, and sighs, and hasty words rattled in undertones. When at last she did step in, she was a little flushed and flustered. She gave a slight start upon seeing her visitors, but the affable smile which she threw at Chris gave him no reason to remember that he was a "Koskuff." And as she and Elva were introduced, it was easy to see that the two women took to one another.

"Well, I suppose—you've heard?" was her first word to Roy when they had all taken seats.

He nodded.

"Everybody—they are simply wild about it," she went on, her words tripping over one another. "Oh, that vile woman! The worst of it is, many believe her and her perjurfied witnesses."

"But, Verne, you don't give her—not really any chance?" Roy demanded, for the first time showing anxiety.

She shook her head. "Not yet. Just the same, my grandfather, he has an old saying: in politics the last lap is where you are most likely to trip."

"Not this time, Verne," Roy reassured her. "Listen. I brought Chris and Elva because they can testify they were both in her shop when those witnesses claimed to overhear him. If you want them to make a public statement—"

"It will do not any good," said Verne, rising and averting her head so as to conceal the trouble in her sea-blue eyes. "Chris, he has two statements made already. If he makes another, what will Marigold say? That this proves still more that we have forced him. Besides, he and Elva are only two. And Marigold's witnesses, they are three. Three lies, they count more with people than two truth-tellings."

"Then what will you do, Verne?"

Thoughtfully she resumed her seat. "I know not. Maybe I will myself a statement make. I have a good alibi. When the witnesses said they heard me at the Concurrent headquarters—at that very time, I was speaking to the Mercurite Protective League."

"How will you prove, Miss Wyle," Chris put in his word, "that one of your multiples wasn't giving the talk?"

"That is not hard. I will some witnesses bring who spoke with me. And now, my good friends—"

She had risen. And the visitors, knowing how much she had on her mind, hastily left. But as they filed out, Chris noticed the understanding glance that she threw at Roy from under her long, drooping, pale lashes.

Just as they came into the street, Chris again had a glimpse of a plump and vaguely familiar small figure, skulking out of sight around the corner of a building. And now he recognized her. He returned in a flash to that day, at the meeting of the Women's Dissidents, when a fat, aging little woman, standing on the platform in a purple tunic, had recommended Marigold for the nomination. Yes, this was Eye-leen Ell-ey-yott, Chairodent of the Daughters of the Plastidome!

"What can that snooping old owl be wanting?" he thought. But he considered it best to say nothing of the sharp suspicion that shot over him.

"I can hardly wait for tomorrow's vote," he remarked, as the three of them moodily got back into Elva's Practigard. "Maybe that will tell the story."

But Elva's expression was too eloquent when, as

he entered her shop the next morning, she pointed to the *Carmine Sheet.*

"Just look, Chris!" she wailed.

This time the sampling of votes had been on a smaller scale. Of 7,316 women questioned, 3,670 had reported themselves in favor of Verne, and 3,646 for the Dissident candidate.

"Good Lord, Elva! They're neck and neck!"

"Yes, but if Verne keeps losing votes, it won't be neck and neck very long!"

"I'm hoping her denial of Marigold's charges will reverse the tide. Do you know when she'll be heard?"

An hour or two later, Verne's soft, musical tones came in calm and clear over the Air Voice.

"I think," she said, after a brief introduction, "that the truth, it is more important than winning the electioning. The truth is that, just when Miss Har-reys' witnesses said they heard me talking to the Koskuff, I was being introducized to an audience by Frank Will-eys, Chairodent of the Mercurite Protective League. I have here some statements by distinguishified persons, including Dr. Will-eys, Mrs. Will-eys, Al-yse Ham-mel-ton, Wall-ter See-moorse, and Margret Clar-ke, the officers of the Society. . . ."

"Well, one thing's clear to any idiot," remarked Chris, after the broadcast. "And that is that somebody's been lying."

"Ah, but to see which side is lying—that takes a mind," reflected Elva sadly. "And a mind—it is something not required before you vote. However, Verne, she has five witnesses against Marigold's three. And most of the votifiers—they can count up to five. So we will see what the next dummy ballot says."

It was Roy who, a day later, acquainted Chris with the results of a "dummy vote" taken immediately after Verne's broadcast. "What did I tell you, old sport?" he exclaimed, triumphantly waving a copy of the *Golden Sheet* as he burst into their room. "Here! Look for yourself!"

Chris snatched up the paper. "Well, I sure bow down to you, you old devil!" he said, as his eyes fell upon a column to the right. "I see you're still leading, more than three to one—"

"Oh, that's not it! Going blind in your old age? There! Over there, to the left!" indicated Roy.

"Verne gains since denifying of charges," read the item to the left. "Out of a sampling of the views of 8,219 women, 4,616 have declared in favor of the Concurrent candidate, as against 3,603 for Miss Harreys."

"See! I knew she'd come out all right!" cried Roy. "Tell you the truth, though I didn't want to let on, I was so scared after that last blast by Marigold, I could hardly sleep nights."

"If I'd been in your boots, believe me, I wouldn't

have slept, either," testified Chris, as he formed a mental picture of Marigold's blade-like face.

"But now everything'll be all right!" enthused Roy, still skipping gaily about the room. "God, but it's been a nightmare!"

But Chris could not help remembering that the campaign still had several days to go. And he had not forgotten the old saying of the Bureaudent, as reported by Verne, that in politics the last lap was where you were most likely to trip.

CHAPTER XIX

On election eve, the bombshell fell.

After an exhausting day, Roy and Verne were seated together in an inner Concurrent office. Somehow, the space between them narrowed; he clasped her hand, and a blush colored her daintily modeled face, and she averted her shining eyes.

"This election, Verne," he said, "it's so much more than an ordinary one."

"Oh, how I hope that everything will come out right."

"Of course it will, Verne. It has to."

His clasp on her hand tightened. He was drawing her closer, when footsteps thudded in the outer office, and she jerked away from him just as the small, round face of Hennery Jon-ess came popping in.

"Ah, I knew not you were here," he apologized, throwing one hand in surprise over his wrinkled forehead. "But I am pleasified to see you. Have you heard?"

"Heard what?"

His tiny gray-green eyes glittered.

"Everything now, it is as smooth as the Plasti-dome. The latest dummy ballots—I remember not the exact figures, but you are both ahead. Again you have gained, Miss Wyle. I think that Miss Har-reys, she will catch not up."

"That *is* glorious news, Mr. Jon-ess!" Verne beamed upon him gratefully. "But maybe the Air Voice, it will tell us the figures."

Automatically she turned a wall switch. The election was, naturally, the subject being discussed:

". . . and so the wagerfying," said the Voice, "it is all on the women's race. The Circulators of this station, they could find not anybody to bet that Roy King, he would be not elected. But wagerfying in the women's race, it is heavy. The odds in favor of Verne Wyle, they have changed from eight to seven to five to two. The odds in favor of Verne, I repeat, they are now five to two!"

"That looks beautiful to me! Beautiful!" exclaimed Jon-ess, rubbing his hands together happily. "The wagerfying odds, they change not except for a reason."

And just then the Air Voice broke out in a blare: "Special News Report! Special! We have this very minute at the station received a most important communicing."

There was a moment's pause, while the hearers stared at one another in vague concern.

"Here is a message," the announcer went on, "from that distinguishified organization, the Daughters of the Plastidome. It is signed by Chairodent Eye-leen Ell-ey-yott. I read it now, in Miss Ell-ey-yott's own words."

"I know that woman!" muttered Verne, her face going pale. "I would trust her not!"

" 'To the mennen and women of Mercury!' " the Air Voice went on. " 'The Daughters of the Plastidome, as you all know, have never before into politicking entered. But now our Directifying Council, it has decided in the interests of world morality to act. You remember that Miss Verne Wyle, when she an answer made to the charges of Miss Marigold Har-reys, she said that she had not seen the Koskuff from the planety Earth. Many good people believed her. But now, on the word of one of the most super-eminent members of our society, we can report that this is not so. The Koskuff, he has recently seen entering and leaving the office of Miss Wyle *by a back door*. Mennen and women of Mercury, in the name of decent government, such treasoning should be chastified. And so, by a unanimous vote of the Directifying Council, the Daughters of the Plastidome declare themselves for Marigold Har-reys for Women's Planicrat. By Eye-leen Ell-ey-yott, Chairodent.' "

A long silence followed. Roy, leaping up, had

switched off the Voice, which had gone on to other matters.

Verne and Jon-ess were white-faced.

"This is the most dirty politicking I ever saw," the latter broke out after a time, in a long-drawn groan. "The Daughters of the Plastidome—they have thousands of members!"

"But everybody," protested Verne, "everybody knows that Eye-leen Ell-ey-yott, she's a prominent Dissident!"

"Why, for Pete's sake, if they're for morality," stormed Roy, stamping up and down the room, with fists shaking, "did they hold off till the very evening before the election so that we haven't any chance to counterattack?"

"Marigold, of course, she is behind all this," concluded Jon-ess. "Three is an old motto in politicking, 'The easiest time to kick your opponent is when he is down.' "

"Believe me, we're not down!" Roy raged on. "But how in the name of all things fair can we answer those charges, with no time left—"

"We can answer them not," sighed Jon-ess. "I myself, I was always afraid the Koskuff, he would into trouble get us. Too bad we rushed him not back to the planety Earth."

"It wasn't *his* fault! Why don't you blame your own crazy prejudices?" Roy defended. And then, turning to Verne, who sat half slumped, fighting to keep back her tears, he put one hand on her shoulder, and soothed, "Cheer up! You've been a game fighter, and you'll pull through yet!"

She looked up at him through misty eyes and gave him her hand, regardless of Jon-ess, who turned away as if suddenly interested in something in the next room. "You've been so great a help, Roy. Yes, with you beside me, I still *must* win!"

The next day was a festal occasion. All work throughout the planet, except the most essential, had stopped; the streets and the corridors of buildings had been strung with gay-colored plumes and banners, and with placards bearing the emblems of the competing factions:

> "Vote for the side that never errs!
> The Party that concurs, concurs!"

and

> "Rather than repent,
> Vote for Dissident!"

Merry bands of children paraded back and forth, shouting these slogans and others like them, and strewing the streets with long streamers of many-hued paper. Then, just before voting time, little groups of men and women began attaching new posters to poles and buildings—posters on which the fresh ink ran in streaks: "Are you an Anti-Koskuff?

If so, vote Women's Dissident!" . . . "Would you
take a Koskuff into your home? Then don't vote
Women's Concurrent!" . . . "Would you give your
daughter to a Koskuff? If not, vote Women's Dissident!" . . . "One planety, free for non-Koskuffs forever! Vote Dissident!"

Chris and Elva, as they stepped out of her Practigard near one of the polling places, paused to observe
some of these signs that had just been glued into
place.

"What the heck!" Chris exclaimed, as he glared
at the warning, *Protect the Home and Family from
Koskuffs. Vote Women's Dissident!* "So they've made
me into a sort of man-eating dragon!"

"I fear so," Elva sighed. "Nothing, they say, con-
vinces like a prejudice."

"But you don't think all this hooey will actually
move the voters?"

"If the Dissidents thought it would move not the
votifiers, they would not all this trouble take. But
come, Chris! I will go to the polls and show you how
we vote here on Mercury."

The election place was a three-sided enclosure
known as the Triangle, at the junction of three
streets, and could be reached only by Practigard.

"What if the voters have no Practigard?" asked
Chris.

"If they have not a Practigard," said Elva, "nobody cares what happens to them, or if they vote or
not. But now I must my place take here."

She pointed to roped-off spaces on two sides of the Triangle. To the left, before a sign "Mennen Votifiers," long lines of males were waiting; to the right, before a placard reading "Women Votifiers," equally long lines of females were waiting. Elva took her place at the foot of the proper line, while Chris, roving about, was not at all impeded by the crowds, which withdrew from him with little shocked cries.

He noticed that a large string "recordifier" stood at the head of each line of voters. It looked unusually intricate, with dozens of spools of varicolored thread, all in constant movement. As each voter moved to the head of the line, he gave his name, which was taken down and checked by the machine; if it proved to be that of a qualified voter, a recorded voice asked, "Your choice, Citizen?" or "Your choice, Citizeness?," and the voter would call out, for example, "Count me for Roy King," or "Count me for Verne Wyle."

"What! Have you no secret ballot?" Chris asked, after wandering to where Elva stood in line.

She pursed her lips wryly. "Secret ballot? Must a person be afraid to stand up and say what he prefers? Besides, if we had a secret ballot, what would prevent fraud? Why, a votifier might promise to one side and vote for the other!"

Too late, Chris noticed that, wherever he stood, nine tenths of the votes went to the Dissidents. "For

Pete's sake!" he reflected, bitterly. "I'd better clear out before I lose Roy and Verne the election!"

He had to wait, however, until Elva had cast her ballot, mentioning the name of Verne Wyle in a clear, firm voice. And then they drove away through streets strewn with the wrecks of Practigards whose drivers had shown too much festive spirit.

"Now we wait till the votes, they are counted," Elva stated. "This begins at the twenty-third hour. Then the Public Informationer, he speaks over the Air Voice."

At the twenty-third hour, Chris was back in his room, where Roy had just burst in with an exultant air, though his tall, rangy form had an unusual nervousness.

"Boy, that *was* an election!" he exclaimed, as, unable to keep still, he by turns got up and sat down. "They say there was an exceptional turnout. Ninety-four per cent."

"Well, which side would that favor?"

"Wish I could tell you, old man. The Concurrents all say it proves the voters are rallying to our side. But the Dissidents say it proves the voters are rallying to them."

"I suppose you cast your own vote, old man. Or, being a foreigner, are you allowed one?"

"Being a candidate, I wasn't allowed one. No office-seeker can vote for himself. You should have heard how they laughed when I mentioned the idea."

He was now out of his seat. "Isn't it about time for the broadcast?" he wondered, turning the switch to "Sound." But for five minutes there was a dull report about Practigard stocks, whose listing had gone up 37/96 of a point on the eve of the election, which was believed to show confidence in the results (the Voice did not specify what results).

Then, for a few minutes, there were statements on the election by political leaders. But all that the hearers gathered from these reports was that all four parties were sure to win.

"Good Lord, won't they ever get down to brass tacks?" fumed Roy. He pushed aside a tray containing some silvery star-shaped food which had come up to them for the Evening Break. "If I don't know pretty soon who's won, Chris old boy, you'll have a raving madman on your hands."

"Have patience, old man! You'll hear the bad news soon enough."

And now the Air Voice boomed forth.

"First the results in the Mennen's contest. We have now some early returns. For Roy King for Head Planicrat, the votes are 2,419! For Roy King, 2,419! For Fred-dericke Will-emson for Head Planicrat, the votes are 711! For Fred-dericke Will-emson, 711!"

"Good for you, old man!" roared Chris, pounding Roy on the shoulder. "You've got him beat to a crisp!"

"You know mighty well that's not what worries me," groaned Roy, turning aside nervously. "You know I'd a thousand times rather not win—unless *she* wins too!"

"Hennery Jon-ess, of the Mennen's Concurrents," the Voice droned on, "he has just a statement given out, saying that the early votifying, it a trend has shown, proving the electing of Roy King. But Loo-ee Wall-ker, of the Men's Dissidents, he says it is too early yet for any trend."

The next tabulation gave Roy 5,445 votes, as against 1,987 for his opponent; and the following reports were in about the same ratio. But it was the third hour of the next day (since the days on Mercury began in the early evening) before a messenger handed Roy a blue thread, which, upon being placed on the recorder, uttered its message in a heavy voice:

"To Roy King, greetings! This is Fred-dericke Will-emson, of the Mennen's Dissident Party. With great respect, I concedify your electioning, and wish you a successful administrationing."

"Well, so far, so good!" applauded Chris. "But of course, old man, I always knew you could lick the stuffings out of any of these puny Mercurites!"

"But when—*when* will they get down to the real contest?" raged Roy. "I'd give a year of my life to know right now!"

"ROY KING ELECTED! ROY KING ELECTED!" trumpeted forth the Air Voice. "We will now listen to comments by leading mennen and women."

The next hour was taken up with the remarks of prominent citizens, who displayed great versatility in phrasing the same commonplaces in twenty ways, always to the effect that they were much pleased and hoped for great things from the winner. Meanwhile, half a dozen messengers had appeared at the door, bringing such huge bundles of message strings that Chris jocularly proposed using them as cushions.

"Lord! Don't know when I'll have time to hear all these." Roy sighed. "Guess I'll have to appoint you Listening Clerk, old man. Think I have to answer them all?"

"Afraid so, Mr. Head Planicrat. That's one of the fruits of victory."

"And now for the results in the women's contest!" the Air Voice announced, after another long wait.

"The most early tabulings," the Voice rattled on, while Roy stood staring at the perforations in the wall like a man about to hear a life-or-death judgment, "the most early tabulings, they show for Verne Wyle for Women's Planicrat, 1,617 votes. For Verne Wyle, 1,617! For Marigold Har-reys for Women's Planicrat, 1,609 votes! For Marigold Har-reys, 1,609!"

"Well, thank God, Verne is ahead!" sighed Roy, as he sank into a chair, mopping his brow.

A few minutes later, he leapt up again as the Voice proclaimed, "We have now some later results. For Verne Wyle, 4,389 votes! For Verne Wyle, 4,389! For Marigold Har-reys, 4,412!"

Roy looked stunned. "Damn that old buzzard!" he growled.

Chris did a rapid mental calculation. 'She's only twenty-three ahead! Verne'll easily overcome that."

On the next report, Verne had regained the lead. The score now read 7,505 for her and 7,491 for Marigold.

"Well, guess she'll make it by the skin of her teeth," Roy muttered. "Maybe, in the next returns—"

He left the sentence unfinished. But all during the time before the next returns were in, he ranged back and forth through the room like a caged fox.

"Now we have some more tabulings!" droned the announcer, after an unbearable new wait. "For Verne Wyle, 10,322 votes! For Verne Wyle, 10,322! For Marigold Har-reys, 10,514!"

Roy groaned.

"Don't give up the ship, old man," Chris consoled, putting a comradely hand on his friend's shoulder. "The old she-devil's less than two hundred votes ahead."

But fifteen minutes later, the Air Voice made a chilling announcement. "Marigold Har-reys claims electioning! Marigold Har-reys claims electioning! On the basis of incomplete tabulings, Miss Har-reys has told Circulators that she a trend in her favor has seen. The uncounted votes, she says, they are in districts that favor the Dissidents. Miss Wyle, when questionnaired, refused any statement."

The Voice ceased for a moment. A numbing silence gripped the room.

"Curse the vixen!" Roy swore, as the Voice resumed. "Hope she chokes on her own words!"

"Maybe she will. Remember, the count's still far from over," Chris encouraged, though he too looked bleak.

The next report did, indeed, seem more hopeful. Verne now had 14,566 votes, as against 14,605 for Marigold.

"A few more gains," Chris foresaw, "and she'll be over the hump."

But the following announcement showed Marigold leading by 18,876 to 18,110. And in several succeeding reports, she remained ahead. Finally, like a peal of doom, came the announcer's word:

"With all ballots except about three thousand counted, Marigold Har-reys, she leads by 1708. Marigold Har-reys, she leads by 1708!"

There was a brief and ominous pause.

"Flash from Concurrent Headquarters!" the Voice went on. "Verne Wyle, she admits defeat! Verne Wyle, she admits defeat! Sends congratulings to successful rival!"

As if a sledgehammer had slugged him, Roy sank down upon a chair, his head buried in his arms, a moan coming from between his clenched teeth. And then, while Chris bent over him, awkwardly trying to give comfort, there came an organ-like sound at the door. The sound was repeated, and repeated, until Chris, mumbling under his breath "Damn! Some more messages!" sprang up and answered.

But no messenger stood outside with the expected blue strings. Instead, Chris saw a jubilant crowd, waving long streaming banners of red, green, purple, and gold. At their head were Hennery Jon-ess and Will-burr Why-te, the retiring Head Planicrat. No sooner was the door open than, without seeming to notice Chris at all, the newcomers burst into the room, shouting and yelling.

"O-way! O-way! Way-o! Wheek! Wheek! Wheek! Greetings to the new Head Planicrat! Congratulings on your great victory!"

Roy sat up, and stared at his visitors in a dazed way. But they were too excited to notice his desolate look.

"With us you must come! With us you must come!" clamored half a dozen of them all at once, as they ringed him about until he could hardly breathe. "You must a great speech make! You must be multiplied! We must a big banquetication arrange!"

Several of the visitors drew flasks from deep in their garments, and, amid hilarious laughter, swallowed great draughts of the bubbling pinkish Vitosan. "Congratulings to the new Head Planicrat! Congratulings! Congratulings!" And half shoving and half pulling, with Roy a protesting captive in their midst, they went crowding and screaming out.

CHAPTER XX

"Miss Marigold Har-reys, she has her plans announced for the inaugurationing. She will a rose-colored tunic wear, with silver stripes and borders, the whole crowned by an orange headdress shaped like a square with a circle above it. She will arm bands and neck bands wear, made of blue, crimson, and amber plastic beads. Her sandals will be rose, silver, and orange, to match the ensemble. Already seventy-five fabricationers, they are working on this marvelous creationing. Miss Har-reys, she has to the Public Informationer reported that the ten days allowed by law before the inaugurationing, they will be barely enough, as she must her arrangings make for her wedding to the new Head Planicrat, which will be solemnified just before the inaugurationing. . . ."

The Air Voice rushed on and on, while Chris stood with Elva in her shop, glumly listening.

"Your friend Roy—how does he take the blow?" asked the girl, as she switched off the Voice.

Chris screwed up his lips gloomily. "About the way he'd take a batting on the head. The poor fellow seems half in a daze."

"If I was a man and had to marry that Marigold," said Elva, "I would feel in worse than a daze."

"The darned thing about it all," ruminated Chris, ambling slowly about the room and rubbing a two days' growth of red stubble, "is that poor Verne didn't lose because of herself. She lost because of me! Yes, doggone it all, the Koskuff issue is what licked her!"

"Oh, but you could help it not, Chris!" Elva came close, and held out her hands, which he seemed not to see. "If people are so twisted in the head—"

"I see that I've done too blamed much harm on this planet," he meditated, as he paused in a corner, with one elbow propped thoughtfully on a large "recordifier." "I've been nothing but a thorn in everybody's side. It's more'n time for me to get out."

"Oh, do not say that, Chris! You have been not a thorn in my side. You have been like a big light."

"More like a whack in the eye!" he corrected. "Anyway, I've got to get out—and so has Roy. That's the only thing to save us all."

She looked at him with desolation in her eyes. And he, reading her unspoken thought, came to her gently, clasped both her hands, and went on, picking his words with difficulty.

"Listen, Elva. This isn't easy to say. But I've been thinking about it a lot. It's been a joy being with you—and a torment, too. Because I've wanted—well, I needn't tell you what. However, knowing I must soon skip away to Earth—"

"Oh, no, Chris!" she broke in, her violet-blue eyes wide with a sorrowful appeal. "Oh, no, you must skip not away to Earth—"

"What else can I do?—even if it weren't my duty to those back there. Here I'm an outcast—a Koskuff. And suppose, Elva dear, just suppose you and I were married—"

Her eyes were averted, and she could not keep back the tears.

"Let's face the facts, Elva. Suppose we were married. Suppose we had children. Suppose they inherited my red hair—"

"Yes, yes, I know!" she burst out, turning from him with a wail. "I have thought of that, too. Besides, I know that Koskuffs, they are permitted not to marry."

And then of a sudden, swinging back toward him, her whole face a-bloom, she threw her hands entreatingly toward him, "But for you, Chris, for you I would any risk take—"

"There are risks I wouldn't let you take."

He did a slow, thoughtful turn around one of the work benches, then abruptly demanded, "Would you—would you, Elva, if it could be worked out, go with me down to Earth?"

"With you, Chris, I would go anywhere!"

"Of course, it's all a big *maybe*. In our spaceship, there's barely room for Roy and me—that is, if we can even get back to it. But if we could go down to Earth and report our discoveries, I'm sure the Space Authority would send a big new expedition up here, including Roy and me. Then we could make provision for taking you back with us."

Her eyes gleamed.

"It would be at least half a year, probably more. Would you wait, Elva?"

"I would wait, Chris, until the Plastidome fell."

"It's a long shot, at best, but I'll talk things over with Roy. We'll see. We'll see!"

His arms reached out, and briefly enclosed her small, quivering form. Briefly their lips met. Then, fearing the surge of his own emotion, he had darted to the door, and was gone.

Re-entering his room, Chris found Roy standing stockstill before the "string recordifier," a muttering in his throat, and a glare in his eyes.

"Curse that machine!" he growled, hardly looking up. "I've half a mind to smash the confounded thing!"

"What's it done to you, old man?"

"Enough to justify mayhem!" Roy pointed to a blue thread strung on the recorder. "Let me just play that back for you. It's from my darling Marigold."

"Oh, don't let me intrude in your affairs of the heart, old fellow!"

But the reels were already turning. A voice that rasped like a file began to bore its way through the room.

"To my Bethrothed! Greetings and love! Tomorrow at the twentieth hour, I will expect you at my home. At the twenty-third hour, we will a big receptioning hold. But first you and I will have some hours all by ourselves, so that we may better acquainted become, and our life together may plan. Remember! At the twentieth hour! Your ever devoted fiancee!"

"Who does the woman think she is?" fumed Roy as he snatched the thread off the recorder and snapped it into two. "Does she suppose she can order me around?"

"Well, old chap, she's just practicing her marital privileges in advance. You'll be there, of course—at the twentieth hour?"

"Not unless they chloroform me!"

"Now, now, old fellow, why don't you go and see what your sweet lady is really like? Besides, she's not going to accept 'no' for an answer. Unless I'm the world's worst prophet, you'll be hearing from her again."

"You know," raged Roy, plunging one hand distractedly through his long flaxen hair, "they've been running me ragged. I had to steal even this minute by sneaking away from a blamed meeting. They've been multiplying me, showing me off like a dummy at receptions, begging me for autographs, making me give speeches, introducing me to every stiff-necked mogul—and not leaving me time to call my soul my own. How it'll all come out, I haven't the faintest idea."

He had rambled over to the window and was staring into the Practigard-laden street like a man who wonders if he should not throw himself out and end it all.

"Listen, old fellow," Chris imparted, coming close. "Elva and I have been talking things over. We've decided there's only one way—to clear out of this planet."

Almost fiercely, Roy turned upon his chum. "Yes? And you think that's easy? You think I want to run off like a damned cur, deserting Verne just when—"

His words stuck in his throat; he could not finish. He swung one arm before him in a despairing gesture, then wheeled about, and strode to the far end of the room.

"I know just how you feel, old boy," soothed Chris. "I'm in pretty much the same boat with Elva. But just consider. If we stay here, you'll have to go through the ceremony with Marigold—no getting out of that. And then how would Verne feel? Wouldn't she much rather have you go back to Earth?"

Roy nodded, bleakly. "You may have something there."

Chris went on to suggest as he had done to Elva that they might return in a few months with a new expedition equipped by the Space Authority, and then bring the girls to Earth, if they would go. Meanwhile, the sooner he and Roy left, the better.

"The sooner, the better!" Roy acknowledged, wryly. "Might as well say that to a trapped rat! Why, the Public Informationer gives out bulletins about me twice daily. Every step I make is checked. They know just where I am every minute of the day and night. It would be easier to break through a cordon of police than get away from that gang."

"Well, that's what comes of being a celebrity, old sport. You ought to've remained unpopular, like me."

"But *you* can go back to Earth, if you want," Roy pointed out cuttingly. "In fact, they'll help *you* to go. They've even invited you to. Guess you could manage the spaceship without my help—"

"Nothing doing, old fellow! As I've tried to drum into your dull head, we're going to stick together like glue. There must be some other solution."

"What other solution can there be?" wailed Roy, sitting with chin cupped disconsolately in palms.

"Well, some of the Mercurites might be able to answer that. What about your friend Verne?"

Roy sighed. "Verne? No harm asking her."

"Come to think of it," Chris proposed, in rising enthusiasm, "we might bring Elva into the discussion too. That girl has a good head on her."

"Okay," agreed Roy, as dismally as one who knows he will soon face the executioner. "I'll send Verne a message. After we've set the time, you can tell Elva."

"Yes, and better make it soon! Remember, in ten days more Marigold will be Mrs. Roy, unless we can think of something clever enough for old Nick himself!"

CHAPTER XXI

The four conspirators sat together on plastic chairs around a green plastic table in the aluminum-paneled reception room of the home that Verne shared with her parents. All looked sober, even grim.

"Well, I still don't see any way out," said Roy, springing up as if startled by some sound unheard by the others. He glanced at his wrist watch. "In just half an hour, doggone it, I'll have to be at Planicrat Why-te's for a Vitosan party. I'd give a lot to skip it."

"Mr. Roy," came in Elva's soft, musical voice, "I hope you will mind not some advising. We still have not any plan, I know, but you should make people suspect not you want a way out. You should play your part just like you loved it. You should even be polite to that—that Miss Har-reys—"

Roy twisted his lips as at the taste of brine.

"Then she will be not on her guard," Elva went

on. "Others will be not on their guard. Or maybe I am wrong?"

"No, you're darned right!" Chris concurred. And Roy reluctantly nodded. Meanwhile Verne, her pale, harrowed face averted, bit her lip and said nothing.

"Now let's go over the whole problem step by step," Chris proposed. "The first thing is, if Roy and I leave the planet, what will happen to Elva? You know what a shadow she's under, for the dastardly crime of being decent to me."

Verne held forth an affectionate hand to the other girl. "You must worry not, Chris. I will see that Elva, she is cared for. The people, they will forget that she was good to a Koskuff. And I—I will like her for herself, and because she was your friend, and you are the friend of Roy."

Chris beamed his gratitude.

"That takes a whale of a load off my mind." He hesitated, then hastened on. "Now back to the question of our getaway. Here's what puzzles me. Even if we could slip off, how could we get to the spaceship, seeing that it lies outside the Plastidome, in an airless, frozen area and can be reached only by a special kind of Practigard?"

"One that is heated, supplied with oxygen, and spaceproof," specified Elva. "I—I see not how we could get one like that. All such Practigards, they are government-owned."

After a brief silence, Verne made herself heard.

"I think—maybe I could help out. My grandfather, he would let me use one. It is an old customing, you know, to lend government Practigards to relations of high officials."

"But could you drive the thing?" demanded Chris.

"Yes, if it is not too big. Sometimes, when I was more young, I went riding outside the Plastidome all by myself, just for fun."

"So they'd let you through the Plastidome?"

"That is not any trouble. The four doors, by a new inventioning, they open by themselves at the pressure of the approaching Practigard's wheels."

"Well, that's something," reflected Chris. "But it leaves a lot unanswered. For one thing, how can we enter the spaceship without spacesuits? Ours were taken from us when we came here, and I don't know what in heck's happened to them. Do you, Roy?"

"Haven't the ghost of an idea."

"Well, I know!" said Verne. "They are in the Sky Museum, under plastic cases. You can get them not back."

Both men groaned. But Verne was undisturbed.

"Our Mercurite spacesuits, they are more better," she went on. "In every Practigard that leaves the Plastidome, there is an emergency kit. This kit, it holds two spacesuits. You can take these and will need not your own."

"All very fine! But won't their loss be discovered?"

"I will a way find to replacify them," said Verne, with a smile. And then, more gravely, "But Roy—

with all eyes turned on him, how can he into a Practi-gard go and be not seen?"

"Seen! And hauled back!" Roy muttered.

Verne stared at the Planicrat-Elect out of moist, sympathetic eyes. And then abruptly she got up and turned aside.

"You know, they've tracked me even here," Roy pointed out, gloomily. "I counted three Circulators following me. The Air Voice and all the papers will report that I visited Verne. I have the privacy of a fly in a bottle. So how in tarnation can I get away from the planet?"

Verne had returned to her seat; her sea-blue eyes had lost all their glow. For a moment, the four sat in solemn thought.

And just then a low tinkling laughter burst forth from Elva. The others stared at her, astonished. But her laughter continued, louder now, in irrepressible gusts.

"I have it!" she cried, between the spasms of her hilarity. And she clapped her hands resoundingly. "I have it!"

Then, while the others pressed about her more closely, suddenly she became serious again. After glancing all about her to make doubly sure that she could not be overheard, she began speaking in an enthusiastic spurt.

Ten days later, at an unusually early hour, the two men wearily slipped out of bed.

"Night seemed a thousand years long," mumbled Roy, who had dark lines under his eyes. "I haven't slept one wink."

"I've got you beat. Slept just a wink and a half," answered Chris, with a yawn. "You'd better be in tiptop condition today, old fellow. Guess you've gone over everything in your mind?"

"Yes, till my head aches," groaned Roy, as he sought refreshment in the Sprayeleter. "I've lived through every inch of the darned scheme till it's all like a nightmare. Heaven help me if it doesn't work out."

"It *will* work out!" promised Chris. "Elva and Verne and me—we've arranged everything, down to the last dot on the last letter i. Too bad you couldn't be at most of our meetings, old sport. But I must hand it to you, you're playing your part. Why, when Marigold stepped in to see you the other day, I'd almost of thought she was your long-lost sweetheart."

"The devil you would!" growled Roy, coming out of the Sprayeleter and reaching for a towel. "That woman—she has the shrinking modesty of a brass button. But I had to play the game, didn't I, so as not to stir up her suspicions?"

"She's so cocksure of herself, she'd never imagine any mere man wouldn't fall for her," reasoned Chris, as he pressed the button marked "Morning Break."

Later, as he and Roy sat at a meal they hardly

tasted, Chris went over the details once more. "Now, let's see, what's the order of business?"

"First that old mule and I have to be hitched up. According to some kink in the law, the Planicrats must be married before they're inaugurated. Now, for example, the man couldn't be inaugurated if the lady decided to fall dead of a heart attack just before the ceremony—"

"You're simply day-dreaming, old fellow. Why, from the looks of Marigold, she's hefty enough to outlive us all. No, old boy, there's no hope under heaven—or, I should say, under the Plastidome—except in what we've cooked up. . . . Say, what's that?"

"Oh, some more darned messages," surmised Roy, as he opened the door in response to the organ-like sound.

Two unusually tall Mercurites stood outside, dressed in red-buttoned green official uniforms. "For Mr. Roy King!" said one, as if by rote. "Is His Honor Mr. Roy King ready?"

"Not yet. What's the rush?"

"We have by His Excellency the Bureaudent been instructified to come for His Honor Mr. King and show him his place for the day's ceremonialings. If he is not ready, we will wait. But he must readify himself very soon."

"Can you beat that for nerve?" snorted Roy, after the door had closed upon the visitors, who remained just outside. "His *Honor* Roy King! I feel more like a prisoner being carted off to jail. Well, suppose I'd better make the best of it."

He pulled a lever, and a wall panel slid open, bringing to light his official costume for the day: a heavy robe of scarlet streaked with purple, with velvety black borders, the whole capped by shining coppery headgear like a huge war-helmet, which towered a foot and a half above his head and had to be strapped under his chin.

"Glory be—you look like Caliph Haroun al-Raschid!"mocked Chris, when Roy had struggled into his grandeur.

"And feel like a stuffed dummy in a museum! Lord, but this is heavy! I tell you, old man, it's just like somebody put a blanket over me, and piled a load of bricks on my head," complained Roy, as he tugged uncomfortably at the straps that cut into his chin. "Well, I'd better be leaving. The sooner we get through this monkey business, the happier I'll be."

"Good luck, old fellow!" said Chris, squeezing his friend's hand. "Just keep your head on you, and remember our arrangements!"

Fifteen minutes later, Roy was perched in an open elevated seat in a large Practigard, beneath long streaming banners, of the same purple and scarlet as his robe. Just ahead of him a matching Practigard, with orange, rose, and silver pennants, bore a haughty-looking lady, conspicuous for her orange headdress and rose-and-silver tunic. And to the rear, in a long procession, dozens of other Practigards were likewise bedecked and bannered. A weary hour dragged away before the procession got into motion, proceeding sluggishly through the streets beneath the blue-tinted columns and the sky-blue of the Plastidome, while crowds stood on all sides in solid masses that had to be held back by ropes. "O-way! O-way! Way-o! Wheek! Wheek! Wheek!" they shouted in a continual din.

The tumult of applause, which rose toward a crescendo upon the approach of the Women's Planicrat-Elect, reached even greater heights to greet the passage of the future Head Planicrat. Guards in green tunics had to restrain impulsive onlookers, who tried to break through the ropes and touch the hem of Roy's scarlet robe. Some of the female spectators showered him with flower-like scraps of colored plastic. And he himself meanwhile had to smile and smirk, and wave his hands to the audience. Long before the procession came to its destination, he felt exhausted.

That destination was the eight-sided open space, the Octagon, nine tenths of whose hundred acres were occupied, as on Roy's earlier visit, by parked Practigards, ranged in concentric circles one above the other, seven stories high. Most of the remaining ten acres, also as before, were packed with multitudes of humans, who were waving long triple-forked pink banners, and shouting uproariously.

At one side, the bannered stone platform stood as previously, with two room-sized enclosures at the rear.

Soon Roy found himself seated at the extreme right of the platform, while the extreme left was occupied by Marigold, who once or twice, when the distance and the surging multitudes made it possible, threw him a reassuring smile. A few feet away sat the retiring Head Planicrat; the Bureaudent and various other officials were perched between. Meanwhile, everything was in confusion, with men and women scurrying back and forth across the platform like excited rabbits.

All during this time the crowd below, impatient and expectant, kept yelling and shouting, "O-way! O-way! Way-o! Wheek! Wheek! Wheek!" Many got down on their right knees, and raised their right hands deferentially. From somewhere high up near the Plastidome, a gong sounded. A loud-speaker burst forth stertorously: "Mennen and women! Mennen and women! Yourselves to order bring. In twenty-five per cent of an hour, the ceremonialings, they begin!"

"O-way! O-way! Wheek! Wheek! Wheek!" the cheers of the throng were repeated. And Roy, with a sinking feeling, knew that the time for action had come.

CHAPTER XXII

A snow-white enclosed Practigard, with dome-shaped blue markings, pushed forward among the crowds of machines converging on the Octagon. Every once in a while it let out a blast like thunder, and the other machines moved hastily aside. Thus it was able to progress through the congested streets, hopping over all obstacles, until at length it came to rest in a corner of the Octagon, at the base of a stairway leading to the stone platform.

Inside the Practigard, three occupants sat in tense excitement. A flaxen-haired young woman, at the controls, spoke reassuringly to a man whose carrot-red hair was concealed beneath a chestnut wig. "Worry not, my friend. All the other Practigards, they must before our white Government car make way. Such is the law. The people, they suspect not. Is this not so, Elva?"

"It is so, Verne. Oh, if only nobody recognizes Chris!"

All knew that the specially prepared plastic of the Practigard's windows made it impossible for persons outside to see in, though those inside could see out. But Chris's wig would be indispensable during the crisis that lay ahead.

"Other times," said Verne, while the Practigard halted temporarily amid a jam of vehicles, "a wig would do Chris not any good; people would know him anyhow. But now they are so excited, they are thinking not of Koskuffs."

"This darned thing feels like a mattress," grumbled Chris, tugging at his headdress, as the Practigard started off again with a jerk that almost threw him to the floor. "What I'm wondering is about my size—"

"You are big, Chris," answered Elva, "but a few Mercurite mennen, they are just as big. You will look like a large workman. But oh, if they catch us not!"

"It's a chance we've got to take," mumbled Chris, biting his lip.

Five minutes later, after several long daredevil hops, the Practigard halted in a small open space marked "Reservified."

"Ah, here we are. Right at the stairway," cried Verne, springing out of her seat. "We must no time lose!"

Chris slid to the rear and folded his arms about a

great plastic-covered gray package, at least four feet high, two feet wide, and two feet deep. It was about all that he could handle, but in a minute he had lugged it past the door, which Verne held open for him.

"I will for you be waiting," said Verne. "Hurry! Remember, one lost minute may lose all."

From the Octagon, a tumult reached their ears. "O-way! Way-o! O-way! Wheek! Wheek! Wheek!" Lines of parked Practigards almost surrounded them. But no one was walking near by.

Chris, puffing and tugging, carried the big package up the winding stairway. It was lucky, he thought, that gravity was so much less than on Earth. Elva, following him, offered to help, but he refused her aid.

At last they reached a narrow platform at the head of the stairs.

"Now, Elva—the key," he panted.

She fumbled in the recesses of her tunic, and brought forth a tiny steel object. A few seconds later, they had entered a small compartment provided with chairs, a couch, and a washroom. This, they knew, was the Reclinifier, an adjunct of the Octagon, used as a men's lounge and rest room, and as a dressing-room for theatrical performances; just to the left, there was a women's Reclinifier. Roy, as the hero of the day, had received the keys to the room and had given one to Elva.

They entered as hastily as thieves and closed the

door. From just beyond the opposite door, they could hear a shuffling of feet and a loud chattering from the crowds on the platform, along with cries from below, "O-way! O-way! Way-o! Wheek! Wheek! Wheek!"

Chris put his package down with a thump, then paused just long enough to mop his brow and readjust his wig, which had been knocked slightly askew, showing patches of red.

But Elva was already stripping off the plastic wrappings.

"Nobody—nobody saw us, Chris," she exulted. "Now hurry!"

The opened package revealed a man's tunic and some plastic objects that looked like a man's trunk and limbs. Elva, working with dexterous fingers, rapidly put the parts together, and threw on the tunic, until the whole was like the figure of a very tall man—all except for the head, which remained to be added. "It is lucky," she remarked, as she worked, "that my job, it used to be with Man-Multipliers."

"Lucky, too," added Chris, trying to help but not knowing how, "that Roy, thanks to his election, could get one of these dummies simply by asking for it."

Just then, from outside, a gong sounded. Elva's face went white. "By the Plastidome," she muttered, "I knew not it was so late!"

"Mennen and women! Mennen and women!" a

voice was roaring. "In twenty-five per cent of an hour, the ceremonialings, they will begin!"

"Twenty-five per cent of an hour!" she groaned. "Chris—Chris, please, pass me that head!"

Chris dove into the package and drew out a head that looked so much like Roy's that he had a momentary shock.

Elva, seizing it, began to fumble with some clips and clasps. But in her rush, everything went wrong. The head leaned left, then right, showing wide gaps in the shoulders. Meanwhile, from outside, the howls of the mob came in increasing volume, "O-way! O-way! Wheek! Wheek! Wheek!"

Chris, bending down, still tried to help, but the unfamiliar combinations baffled him.

"Mennen and women! Quiet yourselves!" boomed the loud-speakers. "The time, it draws near!"

And now the platform door swung open and a six-footer stalked in, crowned by a splendor of scarlet and purple.

"Thank God, you're here! I was afraid you mightn't make it!" he burst out as he quickly closed the door behind him. "I told the retiring Planicrat I had to go to the rest room to adjust my bonnet, which was slipping off. Come! Ready?"

"Just one minute!" deterred Elva, still struggling with the head fastenings.

From outside, the loud-speakers thundered, "Mennen and women! We are almost—almost ready . . ."

"O-way! O-way! Way-o! Wheek! Wheek! Wheek!" answered the multitude.

Just then the dummy's head gave out a sudden snapping sound, and Elva sighed with relief. "Ah, I have it!"

The manikin was exactly Roy's size, and looked so much like him that anyone would have had trouble to tell them apart.

"Now for the clothes!" cried Roy. And he pulled off the dummy's tunic, and substituted his own scar-let-and-purple black-bordered robe, crowning the whole with the huge conical headgear, which he fastened by means of the chin straps. Meanwhile, Elva worked frantically at some electronic tubes and wires, which she had taken out of the plastic package and was attaching beneath the dummy's clothes.

"Mennen and women! Mennen and women!" pro-claimed that stertorous voice from outside. "In two minutes more, the ceremonialings, they begin! In two minutes!"

"God! If I don't leave by then—" gasped Roy.

"You and Chris—go down fast—into the Practi-gard!" Elva ordered, distractedly. "I'll join you right away!"

For the fraction of a second, the men hesitated. But something in Elva's manner told them that they must obey.

As they dashed past the rear door, they could see how Elva's deft fingers maneuvered some further electronic equipment, like a minute radio chassis, which she was slipping under her tunic. They observed how the face of Roy's multiple, responsive to the invisible rays sent out by the girl, began to quiver, and the mouth opened and closed, and the face smiled and smirked in a natural-seeming way.

"In one minute more, mennen and women—"

As these words dinned forth and the applause rose in ever louder waves, Elva threw open the door leading to the platform, while keeping herself out of view.

Meantime Roy's multiple, guided by the waves she sent out, moved across the platform to a seat near the retiring Planicrat. From across the platform, Marigold smiled happily as the figure took its place. The crowd broke into still more tumultuous applause. The loud-speakers roared, "Now, now, mennen and women, the ceremonialings, they begin!" A band struck up a patriotic tune, beginning, "The Mercurite is Heaven's first light!" And no one saw the slim girl who raced, almost flew down the winding stairs from the rear of the stone platform.

CHAPTER XXIII

"If only they don't catch on about that dummy!" gasped Roy, as Elva joined the others in the Practi- gard.

"We'll make a good start first!" prophesied Elva, taking her seat, while Verne started the engines. "Your—your funny-colored hat, Roy, it hides so much of your multiple's face. Besides, the people's minds, they are on the ceremonialings."

The Practigard gave a great leap, cleared a row of parked vehicles, and came down with a jolt that turned it halfway over.

"Careful, Verne! Careful!" warned Elva.

They had paused; Verne tried to decide on her course along streets piled so thickly with parked Practigards that there was hardly a passageway.

Meanwhile, Elva had turned a switch from "Si- lence" to "Sound." And instantly the Air Voice was heard:

"His High Honor the Bureaudent, he will now a few words speak."

A roar of applause followed. "O-way! O-way! Way-o! Wheek! Wheek!" But even above this frenzy, the others could hear Roy's fervent cry, "Thank God, we're still safe!"

They swerved, twisted, and hopped through many streets, took a tortuous way around masses of Practigards, and came to such a jolting stop that only the floor and wall cushions saved them from injury.

Then, while they paused at an intersection to avoid a green Practigard bounding from the opposite direction, they were once more aware of the Air Voice.

"Mennen and women, we will now have a most beautiful ceremonialing, when our new Head Planicrat, he will in holy matrimony be joined to our new Women's Planicrat."

There was a fresh round of cheering.

"Before the ceremonialing, we will a brief word hear from the new Head Planicrat."

"Lord!" muttered Roy. "Now I'm on the spot!"

Uproarious applause drowned out his words. At the same time, Verne started the Practigard forward with a spurt that took them over a mountain of parked machines, the last of which they cleared by less than the length of an elbow.

"His Honor Roy King, he will now to you speak!"

An ominous silence descended on the Air Voice, followed by a wild confusion of sounds. A woman's scream shrilled forth as clearly as if from the next room. There were yells: "Frauds! . . . Robbers! . . . Murderers!" Then the Practigard went lurching on its way again with a noise that overpowered the Air Voice. Speeding wildly, it made a series of leaps down an avenue between the grim, tall, identical, flat-roofed granite buildings. It narrowly averted crashing into several approaching vehicles, barely missed one of the great roof-supporting columns, and shot around a curve with a rush that almost capsized it.

Then, in their haste, the fugitives found themselves face to face with a stone wall.

"By the Plastidome!" groaned Verne. "I have the wrong turn taken!"

The others were white-faced. And while Verne put the engines into reverse and slowly backed out, they once more heard the Air Voice.

"Mennen and women! Mennen and women! Be calm! Keep your seats! There is no cause for a disturbancy! This trouble, to its roots we will soon get!"

There was a pause, punctuated by a sound as of a multitude clamoring. Then, while Verne still frantically backed the Practigard out of the blind alley, the Air Voice again blared:

"Mennen and women! We have some investigationing made. In the Mennen's Reclinifier, we have evidence found of a heinous crime. Some strips of torn plastic, they show that a great struggle went on.

His Honor Roy King, he is known to have gone to the Reclinifier to adjust his crown . . ."

A rattling from the engines drowned out the next words.

". . . kidnaping," the Voice went on. "Her Honor Miss Marigold Har-reys, she too says it was a kidnaping. Roy King, she says, he would never have deserted. She thinks some bandits, they put his multiple in his place, and are holding him for a ransom of thousands of Mercures . . ."

Roy muttered beneath his breath. Chris let out a low whistling. And the Practigard, having just escaped the blind alley, shot forward again more recklessly than ever.

"Faster! Faster, Verne, faster," Roy urged, in a hoarse whisper. "In no time at all, they'll be after us!"

Verne's fingers, as she maneuvered the steering stick, were shaking. Suddenly she stopped, and turned to Elva with a gasp. "I wonder, dear, if you'd mind taking over?"

While the two women hastily changed places, the Air Voice continued:

"The Public Protectioners, they are on the trail of the criminals. Reports, they have from many directions come in. Some say it is a dark-green Practigard. The Protectioners, they are likewise investigationing a red Practigard, with black bars, which, it is claimed, may carry the kidnapers. There is also a yellow Practigard, with purple stripes . . ."

Just then the fugitives saw a long blue wall towering before them—the Plastidome! They plunged
into a tunnel, and soon had passed the four successive
doors, which opened automatically at their approach,
and automatically closed behind them. At the same
time, Elva pulled a lever marked "Pneumatic Seal,"
to prevent the escape of their air into airless space.

"Mennen and women!" the Air Voice roared on.
"The Public Protectioners, they have a new lead!
They are chasing a white Practigard, which has gone
crazy in the streets. It has from many points been
reported, and is believed to be the criminals' stolen
car. Meanwhile the ceremonialings, they can go not
on, since Miss Har-reys, she can take not her office
except as the Head Planicrat's wife. If Mr. Roy King,
he is found not today, a new electioning must be
held."

The runaways had come through the Plastidome
into tumbled ice fields penetrated by a maze of great
pipes, over which the Practigard cast an eerie glitter
with its orange-red searchlight eyes. Above them,
the stars shone in sharp, untwinkling multitudes.

"Faster, Elva, faster!" Roy urged.

Then the Air Voice bore a new report: "Miss Marigold Har-reys, she has an accusationing made. She
says she knows now who kidnaped Roy King. The
master criminal, he is the Koskuff from the planety
Earth."

Chris lurched forward with a low, short laugh.

"Hell! I don't mind taking a little more blame!"

And then, trying hard to make himself heard above the noise of the leaping, swerving, rocking Practigard, "But listen, girls! If we escape and you're found in this car, you'll be held responsible—"

"No, not at all!" Elva's reply tinkled forth merrily, even as she guided the vehicle around a great ice block. "We will say we were forced to drive you. We were kidnaped. Then we will be heroines, and everybody, they will be sorry that through such great danger we went."

"Yes, and I was the wicked kidnaper!" laughed Chris. "I'm such a desperado, I also made Roy go back to Earth!"

"You did it, Chris, with some dreadful Earth weapon," Elva fabricated. "We could resist not. I myself, I will all about it explain."

But the laughter left them as the Air Voice droned forth again, "The kidnaping Practigard, it has been as far as the Plastidome traced! The criminal, he thinks to throw off pursuit for a time in the death world. But the Public Protectioners, they are close behind him."

Just then Verne let out a shrill cry. Her lips drew far apart in terror as she began frenziedly pointing. From around a ridge ice a mile or two to the rear, two orange-red lights had emerged.

"Lord help us now!" muttered Roy.

With long, spine-jarring hops, Elva drove the Practigard more recklessly than ever. She narrowly missed a ravine, and knocked off the crest of a jagged mound of ice. But still, from behind, those orange-red lights glittered, growing larger and brighter each moment.

"No use!" wailed Verne. "The Practigards of the Public Protectioners—they are the world's fastest!"

Suddenly Elva switched off the searchlights and the lights inside the car, which was thrown into a darkness unbroken except by the stars. Abruptly, at the same time, she swerved her Practigard to the right, across a fairly even ice field. She took several hops, while the vehicle rolled and pitched until it seemed about to turn over. Then, beneath a low mound of ice, she switched off the motors.

"Our car being snow white, and looking just like the ice," she pointed out, "they will see us not!"

Two or three minutes later the pursuing Practigard, huge and cigar-shaped and faintly luminous, went leaping and bounding past, a quarter of a mile away. Its orange-red searchlight eyes illuminated long swaths of the ice ahead. Then it disappeared around the curve of a low ice hill.

And while the fugitives huddled together with cries of relief, the Air Voice thundered forth once more:

"Mennen and women! One of our Practigards, it has almost caught the brigands' car. The Protectioners, they have sent out many more Practigards, to make sure the kidnapers escape not."

"Hadn't we better get started again?" asked Roy, anxiously.

Elva pressed a button, and once more they felt the engines throbbing beneath them.

"Miss Marigold Har-reys," the Air Voice rattled on, "she has extreme punishings recommended to avenge poor Roy King. She says the criminals, they must to the Public Executionifier be sent."

"Come, please, Elva, let's get going!" Roy begged from somewhere in the darkness.

With a jerk, the Practigard started tentatively forward, though without head lamps or inner lighting.

"But where are we going?" Chris spoke up from the coaly blackness. "We've got to find the spaceship *Rocket Age.* How in thunder can we?"

No answer came to him except the noise of the Practigard bumping across the night. The lack of light kept progress to a snail's pace.

"Mennen and women!" the Air Voice intruded once more. "The Public Informationer, he tells us that the criminals, they will in two hours be caught, or will die in the death world. In the white Government Practigards, there is only oxygen enough to last four passengers two hours!"

"Two hours!" groaned Roy. "Already nearly one is gone!"

Just then Chris, peering across the ice hummocks that glittered ghostlike in the starlight, let out a triumphant cry.

"There! Over there!"

The others could not see how excitedly he was pointing. But somehow he did make them aware of the frost-covered pyramidal rock, towering to their right more than a hundred feet above the wilderness floor.

"Don't you remember?" he shouted. "That rock is right near the spacecar!"

New hope flashed to them all as Elva began guiding the Practigard toward the rock.

But now their troubles commenced all over again.

"Time to slip on our spacesuits!" decided Chris, as he struggled to keep his balance in the lurching craft. "But how—without a light?"

Elva turned a switch, and a milky white triangular patch glowed dimly—barely sufficient to enable the men to adjust the spacesuits, while they still kept their faces uncovered.

At the same time, Elva let out a sharp cry. From far off, across the icy waste, two pairs of orange-red lights were rapidly converging toward them.

The faint illumination inside the car had betrayed them!

The orange-red lights shifted and wavered, and caught the retreating Practigard in their focus. This time there could be no escape except in speed!

Desperately Elva switched on their own searchlights, and again they went skipping across the ice in a series of long hops. It was their salvation that, from time to time, the ice ridges hid them from the pursuers, who were temporarily thrown off the track.

Then, with a shout, Chris pointed to a bullet-shaped object, a little like an Eskimo hut in the immensity of the ice. And a minute or two later, as two pairs of orange-red lights rose above a glacial crest scarcely a mile behind, the Practigard halted just before the *Rocket Age*.

In a fervent clasp, Roy took Verne into his arms, while Chris did the same with Elva.

"Be back in a few months!" both men promised.

"We'll wait—no matter how long!" swore the girls.

"But oh, Chris, how can you ever come back?" wailed Elva. "You're still a Koskuff—wanted for the kidnaping—"

"Have no fear, Elva!" He smiled at her reassuringly. "They'll not know me when I come back. On Earth, we have effective ways of dyeing hair."

"Then I'll wait—for my black-haired Chris!" were almost her last words to him as, between laughter and tears, she cried her farewells.

A moment later, Chris and Roy had snapped on their red transparent face coverings, which automatically started the flow of heat and oxygen.

Gasping, they rushed into the ice-covered, airless waste, and across the short space to the *Rocket Age*. Two immense Practigards, vaulting over a ridge a hundred yards away as the men threw open the spaceship's outer door, set off the fugitives' padded forms in a glaring orange-red light.

Then the men had plunged out of sight. And a

score of figures, muffled in spacesuits, poured in a bewildered silence on to the ice as the *Rocket Age* shivered and quaked, and then, with a flare of golden flame, shot off toward a bright double star burning low against the eastern horizon.

www.ingramcontent.com/pod-product-compliance
Lightning Source LLC
Chambersburg PA
CBHW031400250626
47155CB00004B/1341